publisher: ODDNESS
artwork: MIKE DUBISCH
editor: CODY GOODFELLOW
colorist: CAROLYN WATSON DUBISCH*

# MY HEROES HAVE ALWAYS BEEN MONSTERS

## BY CODY GOODFELLOW

I remember exactly when I lost my taste for fantasy as a refuge from real-world woes.

Chechen separatists took 1,200 children and adults hostage at School No.1 in Beslan, North Ossetia in September, 2004. Amid the horrors of the siege, one child later described breaking down in tears and praying to be saved by Harry Potter. In despair and panic, trapped in an unthinkable situation, the boy voiced the hope that the hero of Hogwarts would come with his invisibility cloak and spirit the children to safety. Many adult hostages sacrificed their lives to save the children in their charge, and stories emerged of even the terrorists protecting them from the military's insane attempt to break the siege, which would end with Russian forces pouring artillery fire into the building in an indiscriminate massacre.

It would be heartbreaking in any case, but the invocation of the boy wizard seems particularly poignant, for Harry Potter failed to inspire heroism, but only hero-worship, and joined Jesus and Superman in the canon of magical heroes who will save us only in dreams.

Even that thin tissue of empowerment is lost to millions as her continuous hostility towards transfolk has left many readers feeling betrayed by J.K. Rowling, and thus by Potter. Rowling, whose genius for forcing us to identify with the plucky orphan (forget the magic; the true wish fulfillment of the Hogwarts books lies in having every adult you encounter slavishly praise you), failed to grasp how deeply millions of fans looked to her creation, and her, for validation of their own battles with darkness, and came away betrayed.

Of course, we know that heroes like Harry Potter are intended to inspire us to emulate their courage. But they only have to trust in their own magical destiny; their wishes seem to come true at the expense of ours. They cannot and never will save us, even if they can stir in us the resources to face what seemed impossible and survive it.

Which is one more reason why I've always rooted for the monsters.

Monsters, like Disney's many orphan protagonists, are also coldly calculated to win our hearts. Misbegotten, misunderstood, they reflect the ugliness the world makes us feel, while defiantly asserting their right to exist and thrive. Show me a movie-lover who can't shed a tear for King Kong, the Gill-Man or Frankenstein's creation, and I'll show you who the real monster is.

As no end of merchandise also forcefully proves, monsters are powerful totems that let us show the world how aberrant we feel in this world, while gleefully embracing it. But unlike Disney's junk-food self actualization, monsters don't set impossible standards that leave us feeling mundane and inadequate. Monsters, we know, are always nuked or hunted down by angry, pitchfork-wielding villagers, yet they always return, so long as we love them enough.

My daughter scares more easily than anyone I've ever known. Her imagination is a feral force that overwhelms her with the slightest provocation. This girl once suffered recurring nightmares about bats that we traced back to a fleeting glimpse of a scene in *Indiana Jones & The Temple Of Doom* as she walked by the TV. Even most classic children's features leave her in hysterics. There was never any question of letting her watch a real horror movie.

But then she saw Godzilla.

Her first taste was late Showa-era (*Godzilla Vs. Megalon*), with a googly-eyed, marginally heroic Gojira and awesomely obtuse Jet Jaguar, but she was exhilarated, excited because she identified not with the panic-stricken hordes, but with the monsters. She was trampling the buildings, raking the sky with radioactive fire, exerting her power. It was wondrous to behold, and led me to reconsider my own lifelong monster obsession.

I was an angry child. Kicked out of three preschools. Pre-kindergarten juvenile delinquency. Night-terrors. My parents got divorced when I was three, and I guess I was reacting to that. My father was a loving, kind man who was missing an eye after an accident when he was twelve. A monster to himself, he drank and used drugs to excess, and couldn't stop when my mother threatened to leave. My father largely disappeared from my life at age three and died not long after, and I took refuge in whatever janky, half-assed fantasy early 1970's TV could offer. Mostly, that meant monsters, and whenever possible, a Cyclops. Polyphemus blinded by Kirk Douglas in *Ulysses. The 7th Voyage of Sindbad.* The hideous phantom of the graveyard of ships in the "Dragon's Domain" episode of *Space:1999; even the crappy cyclops on Lost In Space.*

My overworked mother was unable to stop me watching creature features all night long on TV, sneaking into monster movies when I was dropped off to see matinee cartoons. At some point, I realized the night-terrors were nothing more nor less than bonus monster movies in my brain. And shortly thereafter, they stopped.

It wouldn't take a Viennese therapist to crack my case. Monsters were my security blanket, my totems. They didn't meekly plead for acceptance from a world that reviled them. They raged and schemed and pillaged and devoured and left no witness unshaken. Even when they are defeated and destroyed, they never fail to show us that the world is a far weirder place than we want to accept.

And they never have. Whenever the banality of human evil seems to triumph, whenever a celebrity or politician turns out to be an asshole, or a creator launches an ill-conceived tirade that repulses their audience, I look to my own cherished heroes, and find them forever unbroken.

> **MONSTERS, WE KNOW, ARE ALWAYS NUKED OR HUNTED DOWN BY ANGRY, PITCHFORK-WIELDING VILLAGERS, YET THEY ALWAYS RETURN, SO LONG AS WE LOVE THEM ENOUGH.**

© THE CREATURE FROM THE BLACK LAGOON / UNIVERSAL STUDIOS

VOL. 2 #4

# ABANDONWEIRD MAGAZINE

OCTOBER 2019

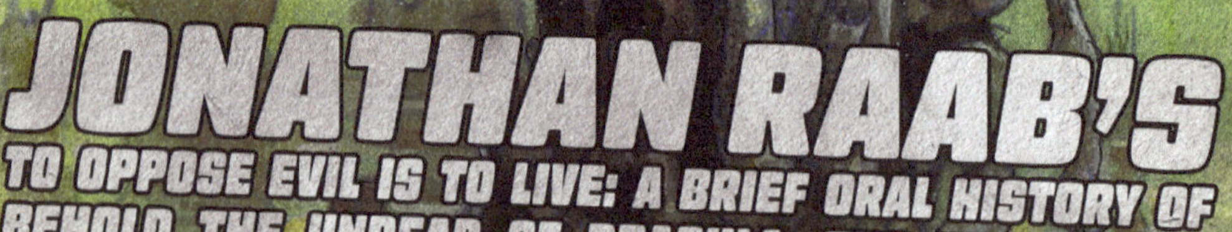

# INTERVIEW WITH ASSISTANT PROFESSOR CLAUDIA MAYFLOWER, CONDUCTED BY MARLE ALLEN FOR ABANDONWEIRD MAGAZINE, VOL. 2 #4, OCTOBER 2019.

**For too long, the infamous video game adaptation of the lost 1974 horror film Behold the Undead of Dracula hasn't gotten its due. Assistant Professor Claudia Mayflower of the CU Boulder Department of English aims to change that—and shed some cleansing sunlight on the forgotten history of a few other overlooked gems—with her new book of lost video game lore, The Undead History of Horror Video Games ($21.99, Uncompahgre University Press).**

**MARLE ALLEN:** What inspired you to write a book about horror games, with a focus on obscure titles like *Behold the Undead of Dracula*?

**CLAUDIA MAYFLOWER:** Some people search for hidden horror movie gems—I'm the same way about games. It's only natural my academic work reflects that.

My mother started me on horror early, exposing me to the best of Vincent Price when I was only six or seven. I have a tattoo of his beautiful face on my right thigh, his ghostly head superimposed over a certain House on a particular Haunted Hill.

Next came the more kid-friendly horror, like *Gremlins* and *Return to Oz* and *Ghostbusters*—*Ghostbusters II* is special, as it's the first movie I ever saw in the theater. I'll fight anyone who talks shit.

**MARLE:** Only positive vibes from me on that one. Wouldn't want to disturb the slime.

**CLAUDIA:** We're going to get along. I found films to love in every era afterwards, from the slasher revival through J-Horror, all the way up to the art house period we're in now. But Gothic horror is my true love. The Corman-Price films, the Universal catalog—especially James Whale's movies—because horror has *always* been queer.

It's the British Gothic revival that I vibe with the most. It's theatrical, colorful, and over-lit to show off those sumptuous sets and costumes; the heaving bosoms, Lee, Cushing, and gallons of Technicolor blood. I even love their latter, exploitative films like *Twins of Evil*.

We have three main categories of horror cinema, broadly speaking, that spawned the modern horror game: the '80s boom that influenced everything from *Splatterhouse* to *Silent Hill*, the Romero-slash-Italian zombie craze of the '70s and '80s embodied in *Resident Evil* and other zombie games, and the Gothic horror of Hammer. *Castlevania, Diablo, Ghouls 'n Ghosts, Dark Souls* and *Bloodborne*—they all owe a huge debt to Hammer.

**MARLE:** Was *Behold the Undead of Dracula*—the movie, before the game—a Hammer film?

**CLAUDIA:** No, it was a Camlough Studios production, which attempted to position itself as the Irish answer to Hammer. But by the time its initial releases hit the European market, audiences were growing bored with Gothic, the bloody fools. But *Behold* is an incredible film, one that transcends the copycat moniker.

Unfortunately, only months after the film's initial limited release, the studio burned to the ground, wiping out their master prints. There's about a dozen surviving copies of *Behold* that we know about, but most are in private collections. A few fan edits like the Moore Cut pop up from time to time. The Irish Film Institute has an original, but they haven't screened it for the public due to an ongoing feud with the British Film Institute that's more than a little political in nature.

**MARLE:** Sounds ominous. What's the story there?

**CLAUDIA:** How much do you know about modern Irish history?

**MARLE:** I write for an online video games magazine, so…

**CLAUDIA:** Right. The official investigation into the studio fire was conducted by the British Army, and their conclusion—

**MARLE:** Why would the British military be interested in a fire at an Irish horror movie studio?

**CLAUDIA:** Northern Irish. The fire occurred a couple months after the film's release in 1974. That's only two years after Bloody Sunday, right in the midst of the Troubles. A couple of weeks before the fire, police were investigating the ritualistic suicide of the studio's executive and his wife, the film's director Macario Darcy and his partner, and Mara Pengrave and Clouta Smithwick, actresses from *Behold the Undead of Dracula* and *Dr. Orlock's Castle of Terror*, respectively. Pentagrams of blood, candles made out of human fat, exsanguination—it was quite the scandal, especially considering the context.

**MARLE:** I love that kind of mythology. Is there truth to any of it?

**CLAUDIA:** Probably not, but it's fun to speculate. So the British Army investigators declared that the fire was caused by an electrical problem, unrelated to the ritual suicides that occurred a few weeks prior. That may be the truth, or it may have been politically expedient. If word got out that it was arson connected to one side or the other, that would have spelled trouble.

You've got a creepy movie chock-full of sex, violence, and occult imagery that presented itself as a creaky Hammer knock-off but was actually far more graphic, *and* you've got it situated at the heart of a violent political situation, complete with potential arson, terrorism, and a sprinkling of satanic panic. We're lucky the film survived the bans at all.

**MARLE:** Did a print ever make it to the states? How did you see it?

**CLAUDIA:** As far as I know, the studio didn't negotiate for North American distribution. But there are some versions of the film stateside.

**MARLE:** I've seen clips of something called *Count Dracul vs. Mad Baron Frankenstein* online. Is that related?

The rumor was that Camlough Studios was laundering money for the Provisional IRA, and that the studio's films contained satanic mind control targeted at wholesome Protestant youth. Many of the cast and crew of *Behold the Undead of Dracula* were Catholic, and Catholic iconography and ritual featured prominently in the film. That's how the bans started, when Loyalist activists and militia protested the movie, culminating in the firebombing of an Ulster movie house where six teenagers—Catholic and Protestant—burned alive.

The ban spread across the UK from there, and later down into France and Germany, although the continental censorship stemmed from accusations that the film's gore effects weren't effects at all. They were really drinking blood on set; the key grip hanged himself during production and you can see his shadow in one of the village scenes; several corpses in the Frankenstein resurrection lab were real—that sort of thing.

**CLAUDIA:** It's a changeling. It's got a few snippets from *Behold*, but they are intercut with scenes from Franco's vampire pictures and set to eerie, ambient noise-music.

The most common real version of *Behold the Undead of Dracula* is the Moore Cut, which I've seen. It's an assembly cut with a bad audio mix, some of the footage is damaged, and it's missing a couple of scenes. Even so, the film is quite chilling and visually striking. You could argue that the degraded image and sound quality contributes to its oppressively spooky atmosphere. It's no wonder the developers at Lyceum Soft were inspired to adapt it into a video game.

**MARLE:** The game is probably the most widely experienced version of the story, at least in the US, right?

**CLAUDIA:** Probably. But I doubt most players were aware it was a film.

**MARLE:** I want to encourage readers to pick up your book, of course, but would you give an overview of the game's development?

**CLAUDIA:** This interview is turning into an epistolary capturing the oral history of a lost piece of Dracula media—I love synchronicities, so I'm game! Okay, so you have Lyceum Soft, a bunch of stoner software engineer-geniuses who made a killing developing accounting apps and web browsers in the first half of the 1990s. Money wasn't an issue for them, so they started developing passion projects—Avant Garde horror point-and-click adventure games like *Journey to Carcosa* and *H.P. Lovecraft's Haunted Providence*. Intuitive puzzles sans the frustrating moon logic that was widespread at the time, gorgeous pixel art tableaus, creepy MIDI soundtracks. First-rate stuff that's been overshadowed by the Full-Motion Video movement ushered in by *The 7th Guest*.

**MARLE:** I've played a little of *Journey to Carcosa*, but didn't get far. The Polluted Wharf section gave me nightmares.

**CLAUDIA:** Have you tried getting stoned and playing? The doorways really open up when you're high. I believe mescaline is the preferred augmentation.

**MARLE:** Maybe next time.

**CLAUDIA:** Sometime in early 1995, their scenario designer and lead artist saw the Moore Cut of *Behold the Undead of Dracula* at an artists' retreat at a haunted ranch up in Meeker, Colorado. They became obsessed with the film. It was an easy sell to the team to adapt the movie—or, rather, what they could *remember* about the movie.

**MARLE:** Why a roleplaying game?

**CLAUDIA:** *Behold the Undead of Dracula: The Video Game* has pretty strong adventure game DNA, with a dialogue prompt system using a keyword bank and inventory management puzzles. The aforementioned scenario designer, Tamara Sato, wanted to create something inspired by Capcom's *Sweet Home*, one of the original survival horror games produced in Japan. She went so far as to bring the game and her Famicom system to the office, and would sit alongside her English-speaking teammates to translate the game as they played.

So you have this top-down, 16-bit style pixel art roleplaying game with adventure and survival horror elements, loosely adapted from an unofficial cut of a cult film. Add in cast of memorable playable characters, a heady mix of cosmic and Gothic horror enemy designs, an engaging turn-based combat system complete with glitching screen effects governed by obscure "sanity" mechanics—and you've got the most memorable, overlooked game of 1996.

**MARLE:** Having played it recently, I'm struck by some of the game's set pieces. There's plenty of dungeon crawling through haunted houses, forests, and castles, but it's the big dramatic moments—which I assume are taken from the film—that stick with me.

**CLAUDIA:** They are. The most infamous scene occurs only a couple of hours into the game, when the party is trying to secure the second of four holy relics needed to defeat Dracula and put a stop to his reanimated war machine. You've broken into the Museum of Celtic History under cover of a thunderstorm to retrieve the Chalice of Saint Patrick. After defeating the Marble Gargoyle, the artifact is yours.

But then Gunther, the Prussian-born burglar-occultist who has been with your party since the beginning of the game, spots the Staff of Moloch, a great gold-plated pole through which ancient demon-worshipping wizards were said to communicate with their dark lord. Now up until this point, Gunther has been a source of humorous observations while also playing the role of thief for the party. But after the reality-shattering battle with the New Forest Witch-Cult—the flashing psychedelic imagery throughout the battle can actually trigger seizures—his mood turns sour. The developers programmed him to spout nihilistic and defeatist dialogue at random points after the battle, and it's here that he sees the pole, says something like "I will see the terrible face of the gods, the only gods that entreat with humankind!" and seizes it.

This is a cutscene, so the player is helpless to watch as he raises the pole in the center of the lobby, lightning crashes through the glass window above, and he disappears in a puff of brimstone. It's fairly upsetting that he'd rather parley with demons than go on to fight more horrors in the material plane.

**MARLE:** A precursor of Aeris's death in *Final Fantasy VII*.

**CLAUDIA:** Absolutely. But Gunther's death in both the film and the game is starkly nihilistic. This is what inspired the game's tagline, which is pulled from the film: "To oppose evil is to live." It's first said by your healer, Professor Phillips, after Gunther transcends, to inspire the party to keep fighting on in the face of innumerable horrors.

**MARLE:** Does that relate at all to the suicides?

**CLAUDIA:** You've done your homework. Six suicides, all about 22 years old, all avid players of the game, from late September through Halloween of 1996. They had all been in contact on a message board, sharing tips and encouragement to help one another through the game. None of their posts mention suicide, but it's clear they had developed an emotional bond. Online friends before having online friends was cool. The police connected the deaths via those posts, at which point the FBI got involved.

**MARLE:** Is there any connection there to the mass suicide at Camlough?

**CLAUDIA:** Depends on which rumors you favor. There's a few shocking photographs floating around, and chances are at least couple of them are authentic. There's also a question of parentage. All six victims were adopted through Catholic Charities, with a pipeline coming out of Ireland which was highly unorthodox, if not outright illegal… but we're losing the thread here. As much as I'd like to tell a tantalizing story for your readers, out of respect for the families—most of whom I've met—I'd like to return to the game.

**MARLE:** Of course.

**CLAUDIA:** So after the party collects the artifacts—the New Forest Grimoire, the Chalice of Saint Patrick, the Spear of Longinus, and Arthur's Shield—it's time to assault Castle Frankenstein.

**MARLE:** I managed to win the spear, but I couldn't figure out where to go for the shield.

**CLAUDIA:** I only knew to return to the Shelly Estate for the shield because someone at the screening had played the game, and *she* got the tip from someone else—that's how these things work. You can use the Baphomet Key to unlock the wine cellar door to the tunnels under the manor. That dungeon is full of the muscle-bound golems we've seen before, just with a palette swap and more hit points. The dungeon boss fight is a team of Austrian Werewolf Commandos. At this point my party was over-leveled, so the only real challenge was in figuring out that I had to equip the characters with silver-plated weapons to do any real damage.

With all four relics in hand, you trek into Darmstadt for the final showdown. Frankenstein's castle is rendered as a mountainside, multi-turreted shadow in glorious, purple-stained pixel art. It looks like a shot right out of the film.

**MARLE:** I've only seen the screenshots, but that giant head, the scientist with the whip, the Bride and that little cyclops—it's quite imposing for a boss fight.

**CLAUDIA:** It's the hardest battle of the game. Arzt Frankenstein's ultimate-but-incomplete creation, Uber-Stein—rather, Uber-Stein's giant *head*—would be a challenge on its own, but it is supported by the others. Kafka the imp tosses status effect potions on the party while the Bride heals the giant head, itself spurred on to attack the party by the doctor's cracking whip. Attacking the Bride enrages it, which is a bad idea, so the key is to take out Kafka first and then focus on Frankenstein. Once the doctor's HP is reduced to a certain level the head will turn on him, incinerating him with the lasers fired from its eyes. The head then collapses into a grotesque

State-of-the-Art
High Resolution Graphics
BEHOLD THE UNDEAD OF DRACULA
™
Licensed by Nintendo® for Play on the
GAME PAK BY
ODDNESS
ENTERTAINMENT SYSTEM™
LYCEUM SOFT©
THIS SEAL IS YOUR ASSURANCE THAT
ODDNESS
HAS EVALUATED AND APPROVED THE QUALITY OF THIS PRODUCT
16-BIT
100 Megabyte Memory
LYCEUM SOFT©

field of explosive gore sprites, and blood drips down the screen. The Bride flees, crying out for her lost love and her father. It's an oddly affecting moment.

**MARLE:** Was any of that in the movie?

**CLAUDIA:** Sort of. In the final reel, Uber-Stein is revealed as Dracula's ultimate weapon, but the plucky investigators destroy it by burning down the lab. It's fairly obvious that the producers ran out of money, as you only see the "giant" head as a composited shadow in the background, half-covered by a sheet. But both the game and the film end the same: with a showdown with the dread count himself.

**MARLE:** The first time I saw a screenshot of the battle, I thought it was from a *Castlevania* game.

**CLAUDIA:** Dracula's character sprite and his coffin chamber take visual cues from the first *Castlevania*'s climatic battle, absolutely. The count is tall and imposing, with a long, flowing, blood-red cape he opens to cast spells against the party, all set before his open coffin and intricately detailed stained-glass windows backdrop. You equip the holy relics and use them against the count, draining his energy slowly but surely. The battle is a bit anti-climactic. He often spends his turns spouting off dialogue from the film like "Man is the true monster!" and "Your hate for one another will destroy you."

At first I thought the fight was far too easy, but then I considered that this was intentional. Drac is exhausted, his work stymied. As in the film, the count's death has a bittersweet note to it. Perhaps we lack his vision for what the world could have become, had he succeeded in toppling the power structures of Europe. Maybe we are too focused on his monstrous methods, rather than the potential outcomes.

**MARLE:** That's pretty deep for a creature-feature video game.

**CLAUDIA:** Would Dracula have been a tyrannical monster, as the heroes believe? Or would he have destroyed the established social order in favor or something more equitable? The filmmakers certainly would have preferred something else to the colonial oppressions their people faced for hundreds of years. "To oppose evil is to live." What do you suppose they *really* meant by that?

**MARLE:** I have to ask—how might someone see the film, or play the game?

**CLAUDIA:** You found a copy of the game. You should pass it along to someone—but only after you finish it. That's the way it should work.

**MARLE:** You've inspired me to give it another go. What about the film?

**CLAUDIA:** Let's see how you fare against the Werewolf Commandos first. The owner of the Moore Cut print is very particular, to put it mildly. Having overcome the terrors of the game will go a long way in convincing her that you're ready.

**MARLE:** Any tips you can provide are welcome!

**CLAUDIA:** There's a certain private message board I frequent. It's a little old-fashioned, but I find that's the best way to approach such things. I—we—will guide you through.

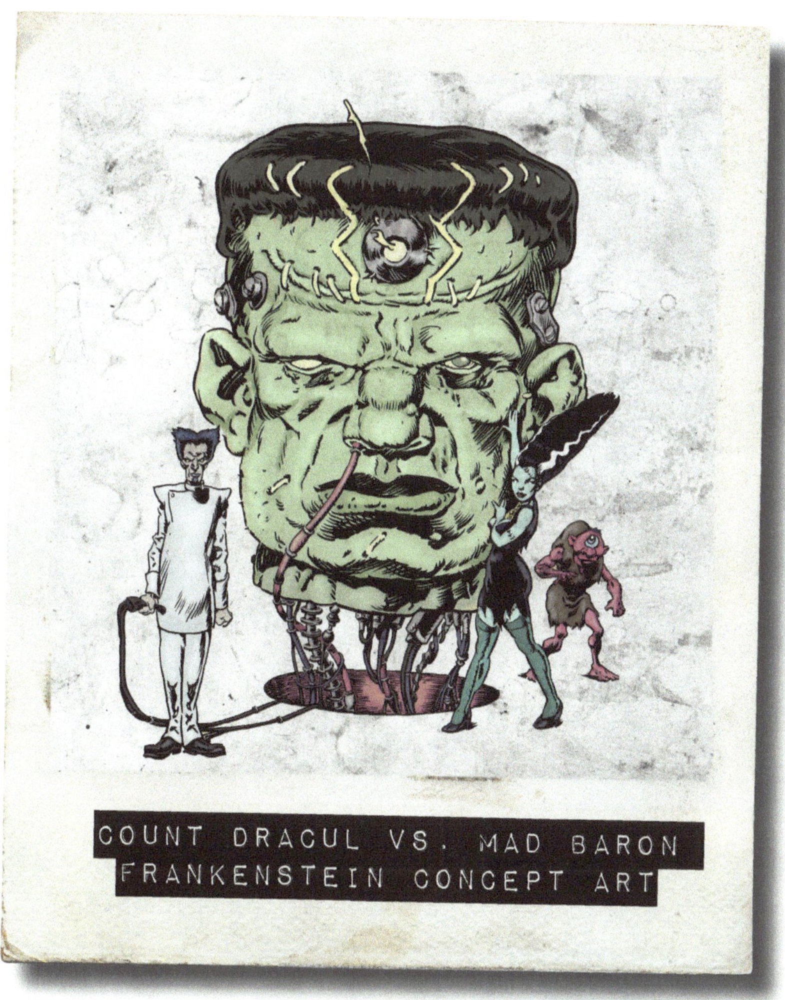

EVAN J. PETERSON
THE PARACHUTE
FORBIDDEN FUTURES 8
12

"…because the human body is unstable, right? Things erupt out of our skins, immune systems attack our own organs, vasectomies reverse themselves. The body is a strange and miraculous thing."

Glasses clinked and silverware scraped against plates. Brandon's date blinked at him and sipped from his glass of craft cider. The kid didn't seem terribly bright so far. Maybe he hadn't heard Brandon clearly in the loud tavern. Maybe he was too polite or too bored to ask Brandon to repeat himself.

Brandon continued. "I mean, you're into tattoos. So many things can happen to the skin, and tattoos stay through most of it. Scrapes, minor burns, whatever." He had seen the inscriptions swirling across Abe's body in the pics on the dating app. Abe was a wiry thing, pulled lean by aerial silks and acrobatics.

Abe stared back. Brandon wasn't so bad, but Abe could tell that Brandon was judging him. Fair. Each sized the other up.

Abe forked some prosciutto chicken into his mouth and talked around it. "Mmm-hmm. I had a dream once—"

*Just once*, Brandon thought.

"—You ever wake up in your dreams and think you're really awake? I woke up one day and my skin had rejected all my ink, just like threw it up. There was ink everywhere on my sheets. In the dream, I mean. Not really. Ha!"

A few particles of food flew out of Abe's mouth. Brandon looked away, but he noticed a fleck land on his salad. He would eat around it. The kid wasn't perfect, but damn it, Brandon hadn't gone out with anyone since the accident. It took him a week to muster up that courage to message Abe. The profile said that he liked smart, chubby guys. Well. Check and check.

Abe was staring at him again, not in a creepy way, but the way a dog cocks his head and stares.

"Do I have food stuck to my face?" Brandon asked, brushing here and there with his napkin.

"You have really nice teeth," Abe told him. "Rich people teeth. I love guys with nice teeth. Mine are fucked up."

"Thank you. My family isn't rich. Middle class, I'd say." Brandon looked down at his plate and picked at his pomegranate spinach salad. He'd finished the steak slices and now faced only the leaves and arils.

Abe relaxed. "I'm new to the whole online dating thing. Late bloomer I guess. I like it so far. It's like a catalog, or a menu. Hey! What a coincidence!"

He held up the wine list and waved it for effect. Brandon nodded and faked amusement.

The server came and went, promising more bread. Brandon stuffed another pile of raw spinach into his mouth. He wished he'd just starved himself instead of letting himself gain all the weight during the long bed rest. The painkillers weren't helping, either.

"I know what you mean about bodies. I'm also a contortionist, not just an aerialist. I can dislocate some of my joints without hurting myself. I can climb through a tennis racket!"

That was flirting, right? Brandon imagined what that flexibility might be like in bed.

Without segue, Abe said, "I was a shit kid."

"I'm sorry?"

"Don't be. I was a shit kid."

"No, I mean—I don't know what you mean. You were a shitty person, or you were into actual…?"

Abe laughed and danced in his seat. Brandon said a silent gratitude that the younger man's mouth wasn't full. Come to think of it, Abe's own mouth was odd. Just a little too small for his face, something uncanny like that.

Abe explained himself. "I was a shitty person when I was a teenager. I got shithead tattoos and did shithead things. I mean, normal kids don't literally run away with the circus."

Brandon dropped his shoulders in relief. "Ah, okay. Because you never know, right? You could be into anything."

"I sure could, Brandon. Maybe you'll find out what I'm into."

The server came back with a third cider for Abe and a new basket of bread and butter. Brandon would just skip the butter, eat all the salad, and have some bread to make it go down more easily. He wouldn't order a second beer. Let Abe get drunk and loose.

He changed the subject. "So Abe is short for Abraham I'm assuming?" Brandon plucked a roll from the basket.

"Nope." Abe cut another hefty chunk of meat and ate it. They watched each other chew.

Brandon decided to play this game. "May I ask what it's short for?"

"Abelard." The boy took a roll and tore a chunk off with his teeth.

Brandon looked down and admired how much of his salad he'd made disappear. "Oh. That's an unusual name nowadays. Like Abelard and Heloise? Is it a family name?"

Abe narrowed his eyes and swallowed. "Not exactly." The educated ones like Brandon always pried. Abe could keep this up for hours, but he didn't need that long.

"Hey, Brandon, what do you call this again? Pro-shoo-toe? Is that French?"

Brandon laughed. "Italian. I'm glad you like it. It's one of my favorites."

**It was a pretty April night,** a little damp but no rain. They walked from the restaurant to a nearby park, making a pit stop for ice cream. Abe was more genteel now. He hadn't offered to split the check, but he paid for their ice creams at the fancy organic creamery.

Brandon put his hand on Abe's lower back as they walked. Abe smiled. Brandon imagined how they'd fit together. Abe was so slim, with those long arms and legs. For a moment, Brandon wondered if Abe had Ehlers-Danlos syndrome or Marfan or something like that. Maybe he was just malnourished as a kid. That would explain a few things.

They talked about circus life. Abe would be in town for another week, then move on to Portland, but he'd be back in a couple of months.

"A girl in every port, huh?" Brandon half-joked.

"Nah, too much work to keep track. I just meet who I meet. It's the life of a traveler."

"Yeah? A bit of a gypsy?"

"Nah, tramp and maybe thief, but I'm not a gypsy I don't think. I thought we weren't supposed to say 'gypsy' anymore?"

Brandon laughed. "I don't know. Nice Cher reference, by the way. You a fan of hers?"

"Yeah, I guess I can relate to a lot of her early songs. 'Gypsies,' 'Halfbreed,' 'Dark Lady.' She would've been a queen at the circus."

Brandon decided to push a little into vulnerable territory. "Do you still have contact with your family?"

Abe didn't answer, just consumed his ice cream.

"I'll take that as a no. What happened there?"

Abe stopped but didn't look at him. The ginko tree above them dripped.

Abe decided to tell Brandon part of the truth. It probably wouldn't change things at this point.

"My family is in a cult, Brandon. My parents named me Abelard after one of the founders of their batshit religion, some guy who supposedly married a sea goddess. They used to make me drown little animals for their fucked up rituals. I have scars on my body under my tattoos from all the shit they did to me. I ran away from home at fourteen and sucked and fucked my way across the country until I joined the circus. Is that enough background? Do you wanna know more?"

Brandon could feel how widely his eyes bugged, the hot blood at the surface of his cheeks. "Oh. I'm...so sorry. Sorry."

*Dammit fuck shit*, Brandon thought. He'd pushed too hard. Who would run away with the circus but someone escaping that level of crazy?

He studied Abe's face, and Abe looked like he was barely hiding his pain. Brandon didn't know what else to say, so he made his own confession.

"Abe, I had a car accident three years ago. I was so drunk that I hit a fucking tree. I was in the hospital for weeks, and I had to drop out of my Ph.D. program. That's when I got fat; I used to be ripped."

Abe made that puppy dog head tilt again. Brandon continued, "My brain injury makes it hard to read for very long now, which is the worst. I hate it. And I know that's not nearly as bad as the horrible things your family did to you, and you were innocent and this is my own fault, but I hope it makes up a little for me prying."

Abe's face held a distressing lack of expression. Then he said, "Hey, kiss me."

Brandon did. His heart raced. Abe wrapped his long arms around him, and they kissed like hungry things.

**They did not go back to Brandon's.** Abe invited Brandon back to his trailer at the circus, and Brandon figured, *Why the hell not*?

The dim light in the trailer came in pulses from the lights of the carnival fifty yards away. Red, blue, yellowish white. Now that they both stood naked, Brandon noticed other peculiarities to Abe's body. *Poor thing*, Brandon thought. *I bet he's inbred. Fucking cultist bullshit.*

Abe was a little too long, yet his chest seemed too short, the nipples too small, his abdomen stretching between the rib cage and the pelvis. His arms continued just an inch or two after they should've terminated in hands, but the hands were dainty. His feet were huge, but his cock seemed too small for the rest of the body. Somehow, it made him all the more fascinating.

Abe pulled away from Brandon's kiss and said, "You ready to fuck me, stud?"

Brandon blushed. "Can I rim you first? Do you like that?"

"Mmm...Go for it."

It was a beautiful little ass. Abe reclined while Brandon crouched in between his legs, looking up at him.

"Here—" Abe flipped onto his hands and knees, facing the wood-paneled wall at the head of his bed. On his lower back, Brandon saw an elaborate tattoo, some kind of pseudo-Japanese mural difficult to make out in the faint light. Underneath that, he could feel scar tissue–a lot of it. He began licking at Abe again, but he stroked the man's back in an attempt to feel out what shape the scar suggested. It felt like a starfish. *Fuck*, Brandon thought. *This poor kid.*

Abe decided to enjoy it while it lasted, but after a few more minutes, he said, "Brandon? Hey, Brandon?"

Brandon stopped worshipping Abe's ass and said, "Yeah?"

Abe still looked at the wall a few inches from his face. This part always made him a little sad. "For what it's worth, I really do like you. And I'm sorry, but this is what I do."

"Huh?" Brandon said, but Abe's ass was already dilating. Scarlet tissue, slick like the skin inside a mouth, pushed out like a parachute.

"What the f—" Brandon began, but the tissue kept coming out and in an instant lurched forward and clung to his face, quieting him.

"Shhhh. Please. Just don't," Abe said, continuing to externalize his stomach, but Brandon couldn't really hear him. The smooth muscle of Abe's gut surrounded Brandon's entire head, then jerked back and forth, snapping Brandon's neck. More smooth muscle came out, covering him down past the shoulders to mid-torso, locking his arms against his body, but he was paralyzed.

Like a sea serpent consuming prey larger than its own head, Abe's body cavity expanded tremendously, the pelvis and joints and limbs clicking apart. The starfish stomach sucked Brandon in, and he suffocated before he could feel the worst pains of digestion.

When it was done. Abe said the little prayer of thanks that his mother had taught him. Full now and lethargic, he'd sleep for a week, breaking down Brandon's soft tissue. Then he'd shit out the bones, but he'd keep those beautiful teeth.

Abelard always felt jealous of the ones with good teeth.

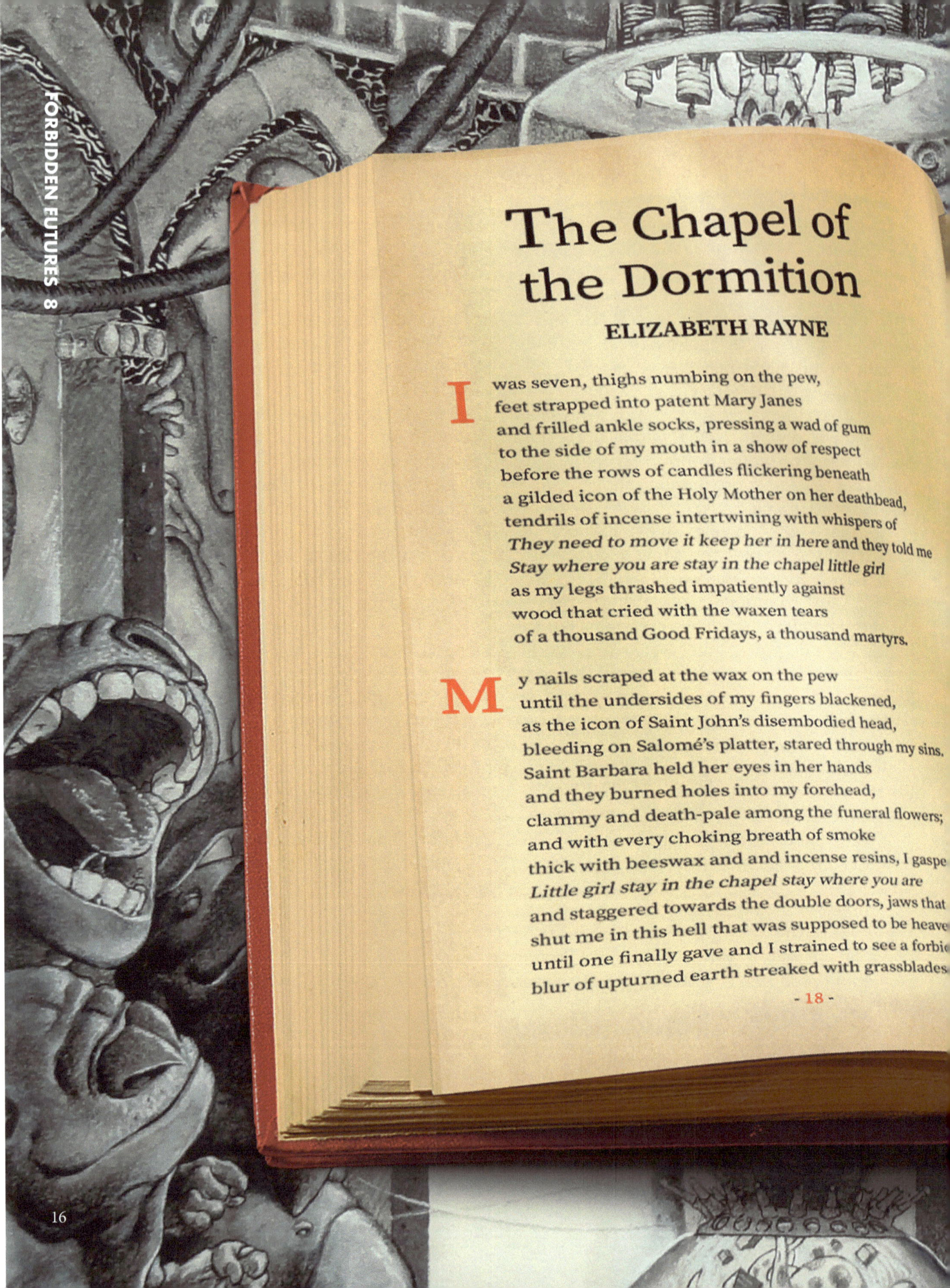



# The Chapel of the Dormition

**ELIZABETH RAYNE**

I was seven, thighs numbing on the pew,
feet strapped into patent Mary Janes
and frilled ankle socks, pressing a wad of gum
to the side of my mouth in a show of respect
before the rows of candles flickering beneath
a gilded icon of the Holy Mother on her deathbead,
tendrils of incense intertwining with whispers of
*They need to move it keep her in here* and they told me
*Stay where you are stay in the chapel little girl*
as my legs thrashed impatiently against
wood that cried with the waxen tears
of a thousand Good Fridays, a thousand martyrs.

My nails scraped at the wax on the pew
until the undersides of my fingers blackened,
as the icon of Saint John's disembodied head,
bleeding on Salomé's platter, stared through my sins.
Saint Barbara held her eyes in her hands
and they burned holes into my forehead,
clammy and death-pale among the funeral flowers;
and with every choking breath of smoke
thick with beeswax and and incense resins, I gaspe
*Little girl stay in the chapel stay where you are*
and staggered towards the double doors, jaws that
shut me in this hell that was supposed to be heave
until one finally gave and I strained to see a forbie
blur of upturned earth streaked with grassblades

- 18 -

y father's coffin caked with dirt, his bones displaced,
anonymous legs trampling graveyard grass
They need to move it stay in the chapel little girl
Forgive me father, forgive me Father.

Frankincense and myrrh smoke stung my eyes,
Saint Barbara's eyes watching from her palms
Stay in the chapel do not move stay inside
pews breaking out in waxen tears as dead saints
beckoned me through cracked paint and smokehaze—
flayed alive, boiled alive, burned alive like the candles,
When my mother in her sheer-to-waists and black heels
and my aunts returned they found me on the pew,
swinging my legs, digging my fingers into the wood,
vaguely strawberry-flavored gum that tasted of blood—
Good girl, they said.

- 19 -

# LAND OF THE BLIND
## by S.G. Murphy

**MORNING HUNT WHEN I SEE HER, TWO WEEKS AFTER OUR LOGISTICS FAILED. YEAH, FAILED IS THE WORD—GETTING YOUR SUPPLY CHAIN ROBBED IN TRANSIT IS A FAILURE FOR SURE. FIRST TIME I'VE LEFT CAMP SINCE. CAPTAIN PARNELL'S ORDERS—MAINTAIN DISTANCE, MAINTAIN VIGILANCE.**

Maintain the integrity of this chickenshit outfit.

I'm out farther than usual—light-thickened vines and packed red soil give way to scrub land dotted with rocky spires the color of sunburn. Two *Shori* atop the nearest tower snap their leathery jaws, peering tentatively about for breakfast, and I go for the long-barreled cartridge revolver at my waist when I see the Mynaabi woman crouched nearby. She's wearing a tattered piece of canvas around her chest and one around her hips, goggling the horizon just like the critters next to her, head-tendrils whipping in a gentle wind.

She pivots her neck in my direction slow and deliberate to gaze into the brush and blinks long and slow, her huge black eye sinking back into the flesh of her skull under the lid like a mud skipper. Reaching out one smooth hand, fingers tapered to fine points, she gently snaps the neck of the shori next to her, sending the other skittering toward the morning sun. She bites down on the throat and rips it out in a great gout of gore, eye never leaving my own, chewing ponderously before darting down and away into the desert carrying the remains in her mouth, tendons creaking, long runners of bloody drool dragging across the dust.

Shit.

"So you brought back nothing."

"If you ask me, knowing the tribe's that close seemed pretty critical to convey. S'why we're out here."

"Leave what's critical to me. Next time you shoot first and tell me about it later, we coulda had some fuckin' real meat. You better rustle up some kinda grub or everybody's gonna be pissed." Captain Parnell rubs his eyes with the back of one calloused hand. "Where's Booth?"

"Doing her job, I'd assume."

He leans out of the mess tent. "Booth!"

From a distance, "What?"

"What you doin'?"

"Beatin' it like it owes me money. The fuck you think I'm doing?"

"Get over here."

She lurches over with perpetual crony Jubal who stands about a foot shorter than her, binocular goggles pushed back on his forehead. She's smirking sadistically, he's fidgeting with a dead radio, no doubt hoping beyond hope to contact our Thracian headquarters. An attempt made in vain.

"No meat?"

I shake my head.

"No Mynaabi tenders, either?"

Zilch.

She turns to Jubal, fencepost grin spreading across her face. "Pony up, short stack."

He slaps a federal credit chip into her outstretched hand. "Chef, you're killing me here."

"I'm not a miracle worker. Stop gambling on our starvation and get in the mess, for Christ's sake."

With their begrudging help I whip up a thick mushroom stew with roots and herbs I've been drying. The tent is soon filled with the sound of clinking cookware as the other scouts soften frybread in the chowder and wash it down with black tea, begrudgingly sharing the last of the salt-cured Mynaabi breast-meat. There's less complaints about the lack of victuals than Parnell implied, but I resolve to hunt a different direction regardless. Lord knows there's nothing else to do, we're more or less stranded until dust-off twenty-seven days from now.

Booth comes with me, a cartridge rifle hanging across her back on frayed leather straps, as we head loosely to the northeast out of camp where the sounds of shori calls and wind whistling through rock dims to nothing as the tree cover gets thicker, the ground softer. We pass the truck-sized hulks of antique perimeter guns, big plasma throwers rusted out and choked to the gut with vines. Something about this backwater's electromagnetic field fucks with most contemporary tech, so they're useless as anything but cover.

The sunlight's down the level of dusk despite it being not much later than noon and soon enough we're wading through a sludgy, stinking swamp dotted with weathered limestone. Insects chitter and nip at our exposed skin as larger somethings splash unseen and in out of the sludgy water. Smells like rot. More than the vegetable reek of your average marsh—more like dead animals, spoiled meat. The sounds of the indigenous swamplife slowly fade until there's nothing audible but the slosh of our boots. My hackles raise and I notice Booth's unslung her rifle, the bore an unblinking socket you could fit your thumb into.

"Think we should pick another direction, Chef."

"You ain't wrong. Let's check ahead quick and then scramble."

The tree cover dissipates to show by the sun-rays of god half our stolen food stock from the supply raid, cans and pull tabs both empty and full piled up in front of a huge rotting *torii* half-sunk into the swamp, streamers of moss hanging from the chipped and decaying wood. Mynaabi men clad in rough homespun tunics hang by the neck from the crossbar, lacerations on their chests, the black eye in each head sunken and shriveled. Two withered beings robed in tattered scarlet chant beneath the *torii* in the consonant-heavy dialect of the Mynaabi, bleached bird skulls bolted over their faces, crooked arms aloft in supplication.

Booth cocks the hammer of her rifle. "What are they saying?"

"I don't know. I never bothered to learn the language of a species we've started hunting for food." But that's not entirely true. You learn a little of something when you kill it, when it shrieks its death-knell.

*Ahkrulik, ahkrulik, bech teyuk khat karu tech!*

With a crack that sets my ears ringing Booth sends a bullet whistling through one elder's throat and it falls soundlessly to the ground. The second ascetic scuttles hooting back out of sight as a second bullet thunders through the brush.

"*What are you doing*?" I try to wrench the rifle from her hands.

"What are *YOU* doing?" she hisses. "That's our goddamn food! It's two fuckin' geezers, let's get this shit and go!"

Something—a twig, perhaps—snaps behind us and we both whip around to see absolutely nothing at all. "You just fucked up some kind of ritual and you think they're not going to go *absolutely batshit*?"

"We won't be out here long enough to find out if we don't get our *food back*!"

Something in the trees around the *torii* moves, displacing the branches and the air in a tangible wave. There's a thunderous rustling sound as something shudders above us and gives a bassy guttural croak.

Suddenly I'm recalling a trip up into the mountains of Beltrine with my father to gather hardy herbs that

FORBIDDEN FUTURES   8

grew in the colder climes. We traveled for the better part of a day and hunkered down in the shadow of the mountain under dusk to rest. I wandered off, as kids are wont, and found a steep recess set back into the rock, like someone had scooped a spoonful out of the peak. The scratched floor was strewn with the spoor of something large and avian by the nature of its prints, rock and straw and shit packed down by bony talon. In that ceiling a dark vertical cave extended up into the side of the mountain, full of the distant scrabblings of something large moving around in a space too small for it. My father found me staring upward, his eyes dinner plates of stress and worry, sweat beading on his brow even in that boreal chill. His attempt to chastise me was cut short by some deep and throaty call—a now very familiar deep and throaty call—and as he carried me back down to camp, I beheld an enormous beak looming from within the mountain's depths.

That same primal weight—that we've stumbled somewhere under the dangerous and predatory watch of something displeased with our intrusion, something much larger than we—sinks deep into my chest. This is no place for the enervated mercenaries of the Thracian League.

I like mushroom soup. In fact I'm especially fond of the idea of being alive to eat it.

"We've got to go, Booth. We've got to go *now*."

She looks like she's going to argue, eyes darting back and forth between me and the food, but a shadow spreads over us immense in span and makes her mind up for her.

As we slosh at speed back towards the outpost, I can't help but wonder how the Mynaabi are going to react to having some sort of spiritual session desecrated, but goddamn my eyes I don't need to wonder long, because as it turns out they're about to tell me themselves.

Our encampment is aflame.

Mynaabi decked out in stolen goggles and night-tac monoculars with blades broken and chipped or others newly minted, cavalry sabers and broadswords—the rest of our stolen supplies. They're tearing the place apart in a whirlwind of torchlight and whooping as half the company attempts to set up a firing line at the back of the outpost. Some crouch at the bone pit behind my mess tent, screaming and sobbing.

Rifle smoke drifts down from the watchtowers paired with the thunderclap of percussion reports and one volley is answered by a massive and instant conflagration—the whole guardpost just goes up entirely at once. I crane my neck, my gun arm dangling uselessly by my side—there's another of those withered ascetics, their entire head gauntleted in a helm of battered iron scrawled with arcana, leaning all their weight on a crooked hunk of rusting metal and gesticulating with one arthritic hand as their head-tendrils flail in some alien fashion. I watch as they curl their withered fingers into a fist and a binoculared scout that could be Jubal crumples in on themselves like a dead leaf in a spray of gore.

Parnell is a dervish, an eighteen-inch Bowie knife in one hand and his empty pistol in the other, slicing and clubbing his way through the Mynaabi, eyes spinning wildly in their sockets. I see him take four individual puncture wounds to the chest before he goes down, spitting blood and hate with his dying breath.

Then, amidst the cacophony of gunfire and tearing flesh, the sound of flapping wings.

*"AHKRULIK!"*

The biggest fucking bird I have ever seen—the mountain-bird, the god-bird—alights amidst the supplicants willing and unwilling of our outpost. It's head is a cavernous thing honey-combed with raw suppurating holes, its wings tattered and streaked with old gore, bone showing through in the late afternoon sun. The Mynaabi bow to it, dropping their weapons and doffing their gear, and some of the scouts take it upon themselves to take advantage of this to attempt to turn the tide. We are met by a scream to end all screams, the cry of Ahkrulik the god-bird, as its beak separates in three to show serrated ridges descending into a gullet that reeks of carrion.

And then I run.

The Mynaabi are butchering us en masse. They heave the corpse of Captain Parnell aloft and worry it amongst themselves, and I even see spits being prepared, though whether they intend to eat our dead or roast them to the glory of their god or some combination thereof I haven't the cognitive capacity to decipher. By the time I reach the edge of the outpost and the rusted guns thereof, a small train has slipped up behind me in the chaos, and we hit the open desert at a sprint canteens clanging, a wake of blood and fire behind. Booth is nowhere to be seen.

We are rewarded for our impulsive flight exactly how you'd expect—by being cast beneath the shadowed wings of Ahkrulik, undead god-bird of the Mynaabi, as it descends upon us maddened with hunger for the flesh of man.

# ERGAMUL

## BY PHILLIP FRACASSI

**TIM STARED AT THE FIGURINE THROUGH THE THIN PLASTIC.** An electric current of anticipation flooded his fingertips, threatening to burst the package apart in some sort of kinetic, hormone-fueled power surge.

His head was cushioned by a folded pillow as he stared at the three-bodied wraith. The paper bag he'd carried it home in lay crumpled, forgotten, on his sky-blue comforter. Next to the bag was the navy-green sheath of the three-inch hunting knife his dad had sent for his last birthday. Express mail from the United Kingdom. Tim figured the shipping cost was more than the knife itself, and could almost see the panicked look on his Dad's face when he realized he'd nearly forgotten his only son's twelfth birthday. Probably picked up the knife during a lunch break—a window display that caught his eye—then paid through the ass for the expedited postage to get it across the ocean on time for Tim to rip open before the special day expired.

He hadn't even wrapped it.

There was a card, though. Of sorts. He'd jagged a note on the back of one of his business cards: Happy Birthday Timmy. Love, Dad. The old man's relief at shoving the hastily-sealed package through the mail slot must have been palpable.

Still, it was a cool knife. Serrated blade, titanium coating and a pocket clip that allowed Tim to hang it off the hip of his jeans. It made Tim—who was a good ten pounds shy of the century mark and a few inches shorter than the average twelve-year-old—feel pretty damn tough. If he was being honest? It made him feel a little bit badass. And that was okay. That was fine.

Tim's other gift, this one from his mother, was the glorious object currently sheathed in a protective plastic bubble and clutched tightly in his fingers: ERGAMUL,

the three-bodied wraith, was the most powerful of all the creatures (in the wraith class) used when playing his favorite game, Angels and Devils ™.

Anticipation peaking, Tim sat up, scooped the knife off the comforter, and—oh so gently—slid the blade between the plastic and the glossy cardstock, freeing the creature from its prison.

Tim folded the knife closed, reverently lifted the freed game piece for closer inspection.

His first impression was that it was heavier than he expected. Much heavier, it seemed, than it was while in the packaging. Only a couple of inches in height, the intricately-carved pewter figurine felt to Tim more like a large stone, or a brick.

"You must be very powerful," he said, enjoying the heft of the thing, the rough edges of the leathery-looking wings, the fanged faces, the pointed, jutting limbs of the demonic bodies.

Laying the piece down, Tim flipped the cardstock backing to read the history of the creature. It was a needless exercise, one done for pleasure rather than purpose, like rereading a passage from a favorite book, or reciting a honey-coated, ageless poem. Tim knew the information by heart, of course. The brief biography written out on the package was nothing more than a brief encapsulation of the demon's full, and far more intricate, history. Entire websites were devoted to its provenance and powers.

Tim had studied most of them. Well. All of them. And he'd long ago downloaded and printed out the Ergamul character sheet, complete with stats, strengths, motivations, defenses and attacks.

"Missile of Green Fire…" Tim whispered, imagining all six eyes of the three-headed creature igniting with an emerald glow and blasting whatever stood in its way to black ash. At its maximum level, literally nothing but the rarest feints, dashes and shields could survive the attack. Weaker characters would wither and die. Of course, Ergamul had other attacks: BINDING TENTACLE was a great one for slowly suffocating an enemy over a series of turns; WINGED WIND was one of the best defenses in the entire Angels and Devils universe. But for the knockout blow, that ultimate kill rush, nothing was better than a level fifty MISSILE OF GREEN FIRE, shortened in gameplay to simply: "Green Missile."

"You're unbeatable," he said, feeling the tingle of his stiffening prick stretch the fabric of his Superman-blue Jockey briefs. "We're unbeatable," he corrected, and moved his hand to his crotch, gripping the figurine tight in one hand while working, with increasing vigor, the other.

**TIM CLIMBED OFF HIS BIKE AND LET IT FALL GRACELESSLY TO THE WEEDY GRASS OF SCOTT'S FRONT LAWN.** He noticed Jun and Scott's bikes leaning against the flaking white post of the Grayson's front porch and felt a familiar pang of envy and hurt. And anger.

The three of them had been best friends since kindergarten at Linwood Elementary, but since they'd started at Mason Middle School it became obvious that Jun and Scott had grown closer, and Tim found himself, more and more, watching from the outside. A bystander. A burgeoning stranger as Scott and Jun grew tall and straight, chatted with girls and played sports. Tim was stick-thin and short compared to his best friends, despite being a month older than Scott and half-a-year older than Jun.

Regardless, the façade of friendship still remained relatively intact, like a highway billboard of a smiling family with the paint fading; the happy grins peeling in strips, the wide eyes pale as corpses.

These days the three friends rarely got together for things like a movie, or a trip to the food court at Banger's Mall off the Interstate. These days they only got together once a week, like clockwork. Every Sunday at 6pm sharp—just like they'd done for half their young lives—for pizza, giant 2-liters of Coke, and their childhood passion: Angels and Devils.

To Tim, Sunday nights were like a time machine. A portal to a better place, a better life. It was like, for a few hours, they were best friends again. As if they were all the same height, laughed at the same stupid jokes, talked about the same stupid shit. For a few hours, despite their growing apart, they settled back into a base friendship that didn't revolve around sports and girls, but around warlocks and ghouls, demons, angels, and monsters. It was about the battles and the story, the

quests and the traps, the vast heavens and the twisting rivers of hell.

Tim pulled the heavy pewter figurine out of his pocket and held it tight in his palm, almost shaking with eagerness to show it off.

Shrugging off any lingering negativity like a worn cape, Tim forgot about his lost father and his care-worn mother, his pathetic life. It was time to ready himself for a night of glorious battle. For a night when life was not a misery, but a fantasy world where he was not a loner, a loser, but was instead the greatest warrior in the spiritual realm. The champion of earth, heaven, and hell itself.

Let's get in there and make some noise, all right? Ergamul whispered in Tim's ear, his three-headed voice multitudinous and enchanting.

Tim smiled and nodded. "Hell yes," he said out loud, and knocked three times on the closed front door.

**THE BASEMENT WAS DIM.** The day outside overcast, graying the high, small windows that typically let through great bars of mellow light around the time the game started, then blackened sweetly as the boys fought through countless dangers during their intense session.

As usual, Scott and Jun were already there. Tim figured they hung out during the day before meeting up with him for their standing Angels and Devils session. He tried not to let that fact annoy him.

"Hey," Tim said, and felt a prickle of anxiety.

Scott wasn't sitting in his usual red chair, making final notes for the upcoming game. As God Almighty, he got to pick the quest, the enemies, and decide on the ultimate goal. It was His story, His world. And he always—always—sat in the oversized red leather chair, the one with the sprung buttons and burnished seat, lumpy with years of use.

Jun was also acting strange. He sat in the corner, tapping away on his cell phone. Cell phones were strictly verboten during A&D sessions. House rule. House... fucking... rule.

But what really bothered him, what made his hand twitch and a cool slick of sweat run down the small of his back, wasn't that the red chair was empty, or that Jun was texting on his cell phone. No, what really got Tim's anxiety creeping faster and faster around his brain like a hundred baby spiders, was that the game table— that old fake mahogany bastard that they'd huddled around for years, amazed at how the huge beast had grown smaller and smaller as their bodies had grown taller and taller... was bare.

No map.

No dice.

No notebooks or character sheets.

No well-thumbed Game Creation guide, the ultimate handbook used by God Almighty to create the storyline.

Tim stepped deeper into the gloomy basement, the single bare bulb hanging over the table lit, but not doing much to illuminate the corners of the concrete-skimmed walls, the patchy brown carpeting, the air of apathy.

"What's up with you guys? We ready to play?"

Jun had the good grace to look up from his phone, a frown on his thin brown face. Scott was leaning against a wall. An old painting of a dust bowl-era clown, trapped in a faded oak frame, studied Tim from just over Scott's shoulder. Tim always hated the clown, and couldn't figure out why Scott's family kept the ugly damn thing. When they were younger, Scott and Jun would scare Tim by telling him the clown was watching him. The hell of it was that the clown was watching him. No matter where in the basement he went, those big sad eyes followed, enhanced by two streaks of black sliding like pulled taffy from the bulging whites down over pronounced cheek-bones.

Fuck that clown. We'll wrap his neck with our Binding Tentacle and SQUEEZE the life out of that creepy bastard. Those eyeballs will pop out like olive pits.

Tim nodded, comforted by Ergamul's strength, his power.

Scott stepped away from the wall, sat down in the red chair—the chair of God Almighty—and motioned to Tim. "Sit down, man. We got to talk to you about something first."

As if on cue, Jun stood up, tucked his phone into a pocket, and sat in his usual seat.

Tim pulled Ergamul from his pocket. He set it down gently on the bare table. "Check it out," he said. "I just got him. I'm gonna play him tonight. I'm gonna be Ergamul."

"Whatever, Tim," Jun said, and rolled his eyes.

Jun had never rolled his eyes at Tim before. Not once. Not ever. It's something they did to other people, when other people said dumb stuff, or made a bad joke. Jun would roll his eyes... and Tim and Scott would laugh. Because they'd be in it together.

Tim reached into his other pocket, felt the folded character sheet. He also felt the cool metal shell of his closed knife, the clip attached firmly to his jean pocket. He sat down. "You guys are being dumbasses. What's going on?"

Scott took a deep breath, then let it out. Tim couldn't help noticing how old he looked. Almost like a grown-up. He had whiskers on his cheeks and chin, and his arms were thick with muscle. Tim straightened his own back, trying desperately to not appear like a little kid at a table with grown men, which was exactly how he felt.

"Look. This is hard for us. But, hell, we've been friends for a long time, and we want to give you the benefit of the doubt." Scott spoke slowly, his eyes never meeting Tim's, flickering between his hands—splayed flat on the tabletop—to Jun, who watched impassively. "Here's the thing... Aaron told us what you did to his dog. We... we saw the body. I mean... we both saw it."

Tim felt the blood in his veins chill and slow. His stomach folded uncomfortably, and there was a strange pressure in his bowels. He picked up Ergamul with one hand, casually studied it. His other hand disappeared beneath the table.

Jun spoke next, and his voice contained none of Scott's cool demeanor. His eyes blazed, his mouth was twisted with disgust. "What the fuck is wrong with you, Tim? You used to be cool, dude. You used to be fucking normal."

Tim didn't see Jun's hand fly at him across the table, but he felt the hard smack of the palm against the side of his head. "Why did you do that, Tim?" Jun said loudly, angrily. Tim was a little surprised to see that Jun was crying. Not sobbing like a goddamn baby, but tears were spilling from his eyes as he spoke. He was shaking. "Why did you kill that dog?"

"I didn't do anything. Aaron's a liar," Tim said, and set Ergamul down gently. He pulled the character sheet out of his pocket and laid it onto the table, smoothing it down. "Are we gonna play? I'm hungry, we should order pizza. Or did you guys already order?"

"Pizza?" Jun spat, and stood up so fast his chair was knocked to the floor. "Are you joking? We're not getting pizza, Tim, and we're not playing the stupid-ass game with you. Jesus Christ, don't you realize?"

"Jun..." Scott said, but his heart wasn't in it.

"Dude, we only play with you because we have to, because your mom basically sobbed her eyes out to Scott's mom, begging us to keep hanging out with you every Sunday. So we did. Hell, man, this last year has been torture. Every stupid Sunday we gotta play this nerdy game with you out of pity. You hear me? PITY. But now? After what you did to Aaron's dog? I'm sorry, bro, but I'm out. I'm totally out."

Tim studied Ergamul closely. He wondered what colors he would paint his wings, his three heads, his eyes. Green, of course. Shades of green. "I'm going to be Ergamul," he said quietly, "and you guys can be whatever you want. There's no way I'm gonna lose, not with a creature this powerful." Tim met Jun's wet eyes. "Never happen."

Jun's expression went from upset to confused. Perhaps even frightened. "God, you really are full-on psycho, aren't you? Holy shit."

Scott stood, put a hand on Tim's shoulder. "You should leave, Tim. You should go home…"

"Green missile!" Tim cried, and plunged the open knife into Scott's belly. He yanked it out and blood sprayed onto the table. A spreading spot of crimson stained Scott's white T-shirt, and Tim's face was covered in a fine mist. "Green Missile!" he commanded again, thrusting the blade toward Scott once more. But this time Scott was ready, jerked his body sideways. The knife pricked through the thigh of Scott's khaki's, ripping the fabric. Tim felt it tear flesh and tried to slide it sideways against the front of the thigh, hoping to slice the leg open.

Something hard slammed into the back of his head. Jun was screaming his lungs out. Tim stumbled and spun. "Green Missile!" he screamed and swiped wildly at Jun's head. The serrated edge caught his friend's cheek, tore the skin below his eye and across the bridge of his nose, then caught the other eye with the blade's tip at the end of the stroke, nicking the eyeball.

Jun shrieked even louder and clutched at his eyes. Blood leaked between his fingers.

Then Scott was on him, tackling him to the carpet like he'd been taught to do in so many of his junior varsity football practices.

"You wanna play?" Scott yelled, his eyes wet and wild and white as the fucking clown's.

Scott grabbed the wrist holding the knife and twisted it. A bone snapped and Tim grunted as pain shot up his arm.

He screamed "Binding Tentacle!" as he raised the other hand and squeezed Scott's throat.

But Scott was too strong, too big. He just grabbed Tim's hand and pushed it to the ground. He curled the other into a fist and punched Tim hard in the mouth. Jun was still screaming, crying. Tim could see him, in his peripheral vision, crawling across the floor. Blood dripped from his torn cheek.

Scott punched again, and this time Tim felt something crack in his jaw. His fingers groped at the carpet beside him. Not for the knife, but for the figurine. For the power. The strength. He fingers found Ergamul, clenched it tight.

We've got the bastard! We've got him now! Finish him!

"Winged Wind," Tim said, but a bone in his jaw must have been broken because it came out wrong. He tried again. "Winged Wind!" he said, but Scott didn't blow away. He stayed on top of Tim, heavy and immovable. He was bleeding badly through his shirt, and Tim wondered absently if he would die from the wound.

"How about this one you little freak?" Scott said, his face reddening around his bulging eyes, his gritted teeth. "Hellfire Torpedo!"

Scott's fist smashed against his temple. There was a pop sound in his head. A flash of red light filled his vision. Tim recognized the command from one of Scott's most powerful demons. It was typically used as a killing stroke.

"Hellfire Torpedo!" Scott screamed, and hit Tim again. Scott was crying—sobbing openly—and his tears fell onto Tim's forehead, cheeks, lips. It was a distant sensation, and oddly painful. Tim wondered if Scott's tears were melting his flesh.

Some sort of new power I don't know about. Something hot and terrible. A melting spell. It's killing me. It's killing US.

The figurine slipped from his fingers.

"Hellfire Torpedo!" Scott cried, voice cracking, and slammed another fist into Tim's inert, broken face. Over and over and over again.

"Hellfire Torpedo!" he panted as he continued the assault.

"Hellfire Torpedo!"

"Hellfire Torpedo!"

FORBIDDEN
FUTURES

PRESIDENT OF THE UNITED STATES
SEAL of the

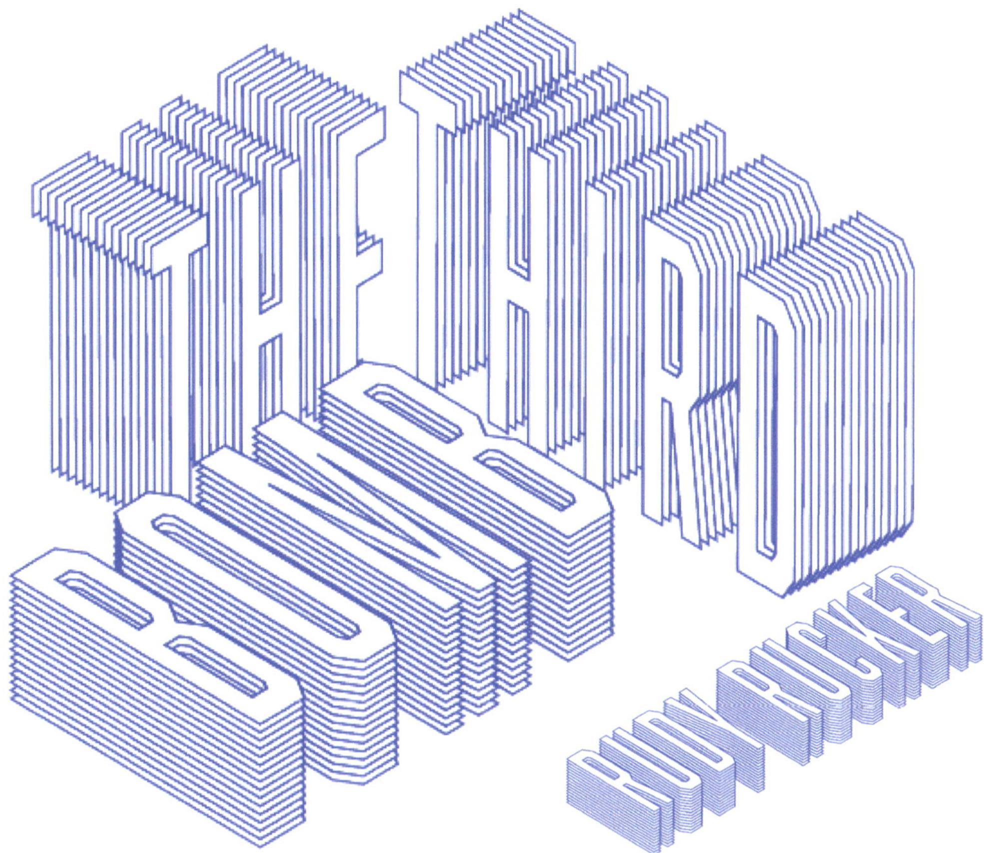



I'm imprisoned on a jungle island. I think it's in the Caribbean near South America. Can you hear me? I'm sending this out live on the Web by talking to myself under my breath so that it makes a slight hum or moan in my larynx. The sound resonates up my throat and into the SWN transmitter that Dr. Robards implanted it in my back tooth today.

SWN means Saucer Wisdom Network. Dr. Robards is the prison dentist. I've been live on the Web ever since the anesthetic wore off. My molar had an abscessed cavity; the man put in a large plastic filling with, I firmly believe, a transmitter inside. What makes me so sure? When I was leaving the office, Dr. Robards looked at me and made the Saucer Wisdom gesture, cupping his hand down and moving it rapidly to one side. I saw this very clearly.

But, yes, maybe prison life is getting to me. Maybe I'm going crazy, sitting in the corner of my cell crooning to myself and thinking I'm broadcasting. Radio Free Me. It's very stressful here, that's for sure. They pipe country music and political speeches into our cells, always with crackling static and unpredictable shifts of volume. It's been weeks since I had a good night's sleep. The ugly noise gets into my head, driving my thoughts.

There's a guy here from Quebec with a really strong voice. Jean-Claude. Sometimes he sings over the piped-in crud, bellowing "O Canada" or "La Marseillaise," temporarily drowning out the horrible music: the grainy-voiced alkies, the cater-wauling prowler-gals, the warbling yearners, their witless rhymes like hammer-blows.

Right now, as I'm broadcasting this, it just so happens that we're hearing the voice of our President. He sounds angry, like he always does. I wish I could blow off his head a second time. Not that it would matter any more than it did the first time I did it. Earth's doomed to become an alien refueling station unless the people of the world rise up together. I'm calling for armed revolution. Moaning into my tooth.

My jailers are fellow Americans. Some of them wear military uniforms with no identifying insignia, other dress in chinos and white shirts. Most of the other prisoners here are foreign. All of us are suspected terrorists, none of us is going to get any kind of normal judicial process. It's terrible to see the United States from the outside like this. To a man, our captors are deeply imbued with the sense that they're *right*.

How did I end up here? I blew off the head of the President of the United States; it was a close-range double blast with a twelve gauge shotgun. I was working as a dog handler for a duck hunt on a Michigan estate belonging to one of the President's cronies. The Saucer Wisdom Network machinated for six years to embed me into this post so I could take my shot. But, sad to say, blowing off the President's head didn't make a damned bit of difference. He grew a new head right away, alien echinoderm that he is.

Now, in retrospect, I see that the Saucer Wisdom Network should have expected this outcome. Far from being paranoid and delusional, we in the SWN have been too conservative. The situation is worse than any of us had thought. Not only is Earth beleaguered by a race of alien sea cucumbers, but the President *himself* is a sea cucumber. He's working full time to foment nuclear war so as better to serve the Galactic Empire's UFOs

The President's inner circle hushed up my assassination attempt. Harry Watson, the guy who owned the estate, certainly saw what went down, but right away one of the President's men gave Harry a light blast of buckshot to the face. The Secret Service took Harry to the hospital and loaded him up with those drugs that wipe out traumatic memories. Even if old Harry does remember anything, he'll damn straight know to keep his mouth shut.

There's so much that the public doesn't know. Thank Gaia I've got this subvocal laryngeal transmitter in my tooth. I've got nothing to lose by broadcasting the truth, that's for sure. I'm doomed.

The reason my jailers haven't executed me yet is because they're busy interrogating me. When my time's up, they'll stage my death as a suicide, like they always do. There's been three "suicides" on my cell-block since I arrived.

But it seems like there's some kind of gap in the chain of command. Rather than grilling me for

information about the Saucer Wisdom Network, my interrogators are bent on getting me to confess to being an Islamic terrorist. Which makes me a round peg in a square hole. Terrorism is square; UFOs are round.

Agent Marc Walladi calls me in for debriefing every day. I keep telling him the truth about I why tried to kill the President: he's hell-bent on steering our planet into nuclear war. But Walladi acts like he thinks I'm either lying or crazy when I try to give him the deep background: about the third bomb and the fizzled tests and the sea cucumbers. On the other hand, maybe he's playing dumb to draw me out. Maybe, come to think of it, they deliberately put the transmitter into my tooth so I'd spill even more. Maybe my signals are going no place but to the titanium laptop on Agent Walladi's steel desk. I better not give out any details about the SWN's inner operations.

It's hot in this cell block, maybe a hundred degrees. We're all tense and sweaty. The hideous country music warbles on; the guards suffer from it too. A passing guard beats his club against the bars of my cage; he's yelling at me to stop moaning; he's calling me names. Idiot. I yell back at him.

"Storm trooper! Sold-out tool of the alien sea cucumbers!"

I go back to my tooth-moaning, but a little quieter than before. I definitely don't want the guard to come inside my cell.

Two cells down, Jean-Claude starts singing "Gens du Pays," a Quebec anthem. The guard goes to beat on Jean-Claude's bars instead of mine. So now I have a little peace again.

A German hippie girl named Ulrica told me about the third bomb a few years ago. Thing is, near the end of World War Two, the U. S. actually prepared *three* atomic bombs: one for Hiroshima, one for Nagasaki, and one for Berlin. The U. S. dropped the third bomb on Berlin after the blasts at Hiroshima and Nagasaki.

There are two seeming logical holes in the story: first of all, the U. S. would have had no legitimate motive for bombing Berlin, as by then Germany had already surrendered. Second of all, it's a matter of historical record that Berlin was not devastated by an atomic blast on August 11, 1945.

As for the motive—it's not hard to suppose that our leaders authorized the Berlin bombing for financial gain, as a power-game gambit, for revenge, or simply out of inertia. As for the lack of historical record—yes, the third bomb was ignited over Berlin, *but a flying saucer swallowed up the blast*.

Goddamit, here comes the guard again. I'm too excited, I'm moaning too loud. Maybe I can scare him off.

"Lickspittle lackey! Don't even think of coming in my cell! I'll rip your face off."

Oh oh, he's getting out his keys. But, thank god, there goes Jean-Claude again, even louder than before. The guard roars back to Jean-Claude's cell, billy-club upraised.

Quickly now. Ulrica showed me a notarized translation of a report by a Berlin beer-garden waitress named Vilma Hertz. Shortly before noon on August 11, 1945, Hertz was on break, smoking a cigarette and staring up at the sky from the shade of a chestnut tree. A USA B-29 Superfortress was droning high overhead. Hertz spotted a black object dropping from the plane. Just as she formed the thought that the object might be a bomb, it bloomed into a pinpoint of blazing light. But a moment after that, a silvery disk swept across the sky to envelop the burgeoning explosion.

Yes! A UFO ate the third bomb. The aliens were on the spot and ready for it; they'd been alerted by the Hiroshima and Nagasaki blasts of August 6 and 9. And *why* did the alien craft swallow the blast? Obviously they use nuclear blasts for fuel. Oh shit, the guard is back.

"Leave me alone, you monkey redneck! I'll moan all I want. You want me to throw my slops at you?"

Gaia help me, he's coming in. He's holding—are those pliers? He knows about my special tooth! Walladi doesn't like the information I'm sending out!

Listen fast now. UFOs are very commonly sighted near nuclear test sites. The army shot down a couple of the saucers, everyone knows that sea cucumber aliens are preserved in Area 51. Here's something new: the government hushes up the fact that most of the above-ground nuclear tests have been duds. The blasts were soaked up by the saucers, and *that's* why they went to underground tests.

"Get away from me, you filthy animal! I'll kill you!"

The UFOs want a regular series of blasts taking place in Earth's open air and that's why they want unending nuclear war. That's why we have a so-called war president in office! He's not a human being! He's an alien sea cucumber!

Oh no, here come the pliers! Rise up for peace, people of the earth! Rise up!

I wrote "The Third Bomb" late in 2006, during the sour, waning years of the final George Bush administration, shortly after Vice-President Dick Cheney had shot one of his hunting partners in the face. I cast the story in the mode of a tale told by an unreliable and possibly insane narrator. I felt free to write such a strongly political story because I knew I could publish it in my then-popular free online webzine, *Flurb #2*. It's also in my collection *Complete Stories*. The *Flurb* zine no longer exists, but you can read all the issues online at flurb.rudyrucker.com. I'm happy to see "The Third Bomb" rise from the underworld to appear in a legit heir to *Flurb*—the utterly gnarly *Forbidden Futures*, complete with an incendiary illo by my fellow Bummersburg State Mental Hospital resident, Mike Dubisch. And thanks to Cody Goodfellow for inviting me in.

ODDNESS
COLLECTION
No. 11
SEPTEMBER
15¢
EXCLUSIVE EDITION
THE NICHOLS DEFENSE
BRIAN EVENSON
NEW ADVENTURES!
68 PAGES

**001. THE VESSEL HAD BEEN, FOR THE MOST PART, DESTROYED.** The impact of the crash had shattered the hull, killing almost everyone on board. All those awake were vaporized. Most who were stored frozen were killed too: the cryospheres in the forward storage compartment were all gone, melted to a slurry. Those in the central compartment had slammed into each another, splitting or cracking so that those inside thawed too quickly and went wriggling and gasping to their deaths. But a few in the aft compartment, because of the way a section of hull had remained intact just long enough, had been cushioned sufficiently for the cryospheres to survive unbroken and to disengage in a normal fashion.

Out of the seven hundred aboard, only three were left alive. These three came shivering back to consciousness. They flipped their insides out and extruded the synthetic goo that had cushioned their vitals and then flipped them back inside again. And then they began, slowly, to palpate the ground around their spheres, searching for the other two minds they sensed to be near. Quickly each grew a slick temporary stalk with visual receptors atop it. The receptors were crude, but were good enough for them to understand what had happened, that the vessel was destroyed, that everyone else was dead.

They slid and oozed toward one another. When the first found a pedipalp or tentacle belonging to one of the other two, it twined around it and was twined around in turn, a viscous communicative slime beginning to adhere them.

This first was called Ch'rgak, the "Ch" and the apostrophe serving as an honorific and an indication of both rank and age. Twining its tentacle around it, another, named Chifi, knew immediately that it and Ch'rgak were not of equal rank or age, and expected to be rejected by Ch'rgak. True, for a moment Ch'rgak's tentacle stiffened and grew dry. Chifi was just preparing to withdraw in shame when, to Chifi's surprise, the tentacle responded. Ch'rgak would accept Ch'ifi! This was an honor, and no small thing.

Twining together, they pooled enough energy to extrude temporary appendages of locomotion. These would carry them away from the crash site and allow them, working in concert, to find a host, something or someone whose mental apparatus they could appropriate, something or someone they could hollow out and feed upon and fill with their nymphs.

A moment late the developing Ch'rgak/Chifi creature was touched by the tentacle or pedipalp of the third and final survivor. A tentacle that had originally belonged to Ch'rgak was first to be touched. Chifi felt suddenly rushing through its mind the disgust Chr'gak felt and which, now that they were neurally connected, Chifi couldn't help but feel as well. A wave of nausea swept through Chifi and he had to resist turning himself inside out. This time, there was no unstiffening of Ch'rgak's tentacle and no subsequent lubricity.

For a moment more, the third creature probed clumsily, either not knowing it had been rejected or not caring. But then, finally, it recognized the judgment against it, and it too stiffened and withdrew in shame.

It took the Ch'rgak/Ch'ifi creature some time to weave together its neural nets, and more time to grow the temporary appendages it needed. But finally, after the ground upon which the vessel had crashed had been washed by daylight and then fallen into darkness again and then ignited by daylight once more, the process was complete. The creature struggled to a flopping semi-erect posture and began to lurch away, leaving the final survivor alone.

**WHAT OF THIS FINAL SURVIVOR?** It had no honorific, nothing to indicate its age or its status in what it was called, largely because it had no status and hardly any age. It was a being of no account—which was why the other two, despite the fact that three would surely do better in this new world than two, chose not to meld with it. It was called Crak, which is hardly a name at all—not even a single apostrophe, let alone an initiatory "Ch." This Crak was a creature of no consequence, worthy of being ignored.

And yet, despite all this, soon Crak will be the only one of the three worth following.

**002. THE CH'RGAK/CHIFI CREATURE STUMBLED AWAY FROM THE CRASH SITE, SLIDING AND STEPPING AS BEST AS IT COULD, LOOKING FOR A HOST.** When it stumbled across the creature known locally as *bear*, it believed it had found what it sought.

Before being frozen for the journey, Ch'rgak had embedded within its cortex a lexicon of the local dialects, and it now shared this with Chifi, who quickly absorbed it as well. The individual known as "bear", they realized, communicated primitively, expelling air to create sound and speak. Bear spoke in a combination of grunts and growls and roars which, with a little effort, could be synthesized by the Ch'rgak/Chifi creature.

The bear stared at the Ch'rgak/Chifi creature without moving.

Ch'rgak commanded Chifi to secrete a new orifice that would accommodate such sounds, and Chifi set about doing so.

*You will secrete it and then you will turn the orifice over to me for deployment,* said Ch'rgak. *I will be the one to proffer the individual known as "bear" the communicative "sounds".*

Chifi wanted to make the sounds, to experience the novelty of expressing itself in this medium of expelled air, but it had to give way to Ch'rgak's authority. Still, as Chifi secreted the orifice it also walled off a small portion of its mind and body from Ch'rgak's awareness and began to secrete an additional orifice there, one Chifi might employ on its own.

By now the bear was ignoring them. It stood on its hind legs and thrust its face into a bush covered with tiny black globules. It began to insert these into its forward orifice and make them disappear. *Perhaps this was another form of communication?* speculated Ch'rgak. *One masticatory in nature?* But searching its lexicon, Ch'rgak found no mention of such a means of communication. Perhaps the bear's action had another purpose.

By the time the communicative orifice was secreted and functional, the bear had begun to wander away. Ch'rgak quickly seized mental possession of the orifice and began to speak.

*Creature known as bear!* it said, or thought it said. *We come from afar to salute you, and to offer you the opportunity to commune with us! This is a privilege we do not extend to just anybody! What an honor to you to be invited to become our vehicle and thus to serve in our inevitable conquering of your world!*

The bear stared.

*Does bear not understand?* Ch'rgak asked Chifi.

*It appears not,* said Chifi. *Perhaps your lexicon is faulty.*

*The lexicon is not faulty!* said Ch'rgak, offended at the suggestion. *It is the creature known as bear that is faulty.*

*Perhaps your rendering is faulty. Let me try,* said Chifi.

*No,* said Ch'rgak. *I will not release control of the orifice.*

But Chifi had already begun to speak through his secret orifice, which, formed covertly and in haste, was malformed.

*Creature known as bear,* Chifi said, *we command you to bow down and acknowledge our mastery. Creature known as bear, obey!*

*How are you communicating?* asked Ch'rgak. *Do you have a secret orifice you are hiding from me.*

*Just an orifice I had forgotten about,* lied Chifi. And then, quickly, *Look, this time the creature known as bear understands!*

In fact, the bear understood all too well. A moment later it had torn the Ch'rgak/Chifi creature to pieces and thoroughly exterminated it.

**003. THE HOPE OF THE SPECIES WAS THUS LEFT TO REST ON THE SHOULDERS OF CRAK, IF CRAK HAD SHOULDERS (CRAK DID NOT):** a creature barely free of the nest, a creature not of noble lineage. Not Ch'rak nor even Chrak, but simply Crak.

For the moment Crak simply lay like a puddle of tentacles and pedipalps and feelers near where it had fallen free of its cryosphere. It had been rejected by the being known as Ch'rgak and, to a lesser degree, by the being known as Chifi. Now it was alone. Brought along only as a worker-slave for those of noble lineage, Crak had few skills. It did not know yet, for instance, how to extrude appendages, beyond the single stalk with visual organs it had already managed to extrude. Unlike the other two, it did not know how to grow appendages of locomotion.

With great effort, Crak began to flow across the ground, moving away from the crash site. It would move for as long as it could, until it was nearly out of energy. And then it would fold up on itself and go dormant. Perhaps in time something would find and prod

Crak and it would awaken and flash into motion and make its discoverer its host. Until then, Crak would have to bide its time and wait.

It traveled for quite some time, through several cycles of night and day, oozing onward. By that time it was, perhaps, fifty yards from the crash site. It pulled all of its tentacles into its central body and subsided into a jellylike stasis.

**004. SEVERAL DAYS BEFORE, A MAN NAMED NICHOLS HAD SEEN A FLASH AND FELT A SHOCK ON HIS WAY BACK FROM THE TOWN BAR A LITTLE PAST CLOSING TIME.** He had been stumbling drunk at the time, and the streak of light and the flash had blinded him temporarily and caused him to veer off into the bushes and fall. At first, he'd tried to struggle up, but after a while he gave this up as a bad job and simply passed out.

He woke up the next morning because his leg was hurting. It was McAlester, kicking his ankle—which was the only part of him still on the path. Nichols groaned, sat up.

"You slept here?" McAlester said.

Nichols looked around. "Looks so," he said. He groaned. "Got a drink?"

McAlester shook his head. "It's almost seven in the morning. You're going to be late."

Nichols groaned again. He heaved himself up and stumbled back to the bunkhouse he shared with the other miners. He dug his spare bottle of whiskey out of his locker and employed it to take the edge off. Then he grabbed his helmet, his goggles, his pack, his sonic displacer, and hurried to catch up with the others.

They were about two-hundred feet down. McAlester had Nichols out in front, slowly shaving off the wall with the displacer, trying to find a productive vein. Smith and Wesley took each shaving as it fell and ran it through the processor then shouted out advice on where to shave next. Bates and Wills worked on constructing and jamming in supports. McAlester meanwhile just watched.

He'd shaved about three new feet before he began to remember, vaguely, what he'd seen the night before. A streak of light. A flash, strong, probably not a long way away. Had he really seen it? Maybe that was just his optic nerves misfiring in the darkness or from the liquor.

But what about the shock? You couldn't *see* a shock.

"You notice a streak of light and flash last night?" he asked Smith, shouting over the noise of the processor.

"A what?" Smith shouted back.

"A flash!"

Smith wrinkled his forehead and shook his head. Smith passed the question along to Wesley, but he just shook his head too and shrugged.

Suddenly McAlester was there beside Nichols, grabbing his arm. "Get back to the wall!" McAlester shouted into his ear.

"I was just asking about—"

"Get back to shaving or I write you up!"

Shaking his aching head, Nichols got back to the wall.

By the end of the shift, he was thirsty enough that he had forgotten completely about the flash.

**BUT HE REMEMBERED LATER, ONCE HE WAS AT THE BAR.** He'd only had a few, a half dozen or so. Hard to remember exactly, but not too many anyway. Just the normal amount.

There'd been a streak of light, he remembered. Then a flash, a big one. Then the ground shuddered. Maybe a meteor, he thought. Weren't there rare and valuable minerals in meteors? Space gems? You bet there were. He knew basically where it had landed, and probably there was a big crater where it had struck. What he should do is go and get it and then, when McAlester wasn't looking, slip it into the processor, see what he'd got, take it, sell it on the black market, make himself a little extra cash.

Yes, that was exactly what he was going to do. Yes, he would, yes. After just one more drink.

But by the time he left the bar, he was hardly even sure who he was, let alone ready to search for something that might or might not be a meteor.

**005. PROBABLY IT WOULD HAVE CONTINUED LIKE THAT FOR SEVERAL WEEKS OR UNTIL NICHOLS FORGOT ABOUT THE STREAK OF LIGHT AND THE FLASH, BUT THE MINE WASN'T PAYING OUT LIKE IT SHOULD.** Nichols realized he'd soon be short of cash and unable to spend his evenings at the bar. The third day, instead of going to the bar after his shift, he had the discipline not to go to the bar. Instead he got the rest of his bottle of whiskey out from his locker and set off to find the meteor.

It had struck somewhere over the ridge, he knew. Not too close to town, but not all that far. Probably an hour or two on foot at most. He took a drink and started off.

By the time he hit the top of the ridge, half the bottle was gone and it was starting to get dark. In the twilight, he could see the impact site, the way the ground looked like it had been burnt and peeled away. It wasn't a meteor. It was something else, something artificial—like a plane crash. But if it had been a plane crash, why wasn't anybody out looking for it?

And wasn't it too big for a plane? What could it be?

He started down toward it.

**WHEN HE REACHED THE SITE FIFTEEN MINUTES OR SO LATER, HE HAD TO USE HIS FLASHLIGHT TO SEE.** Wreckage was everywhere, along with strange, broken metallic eggs and bits of mechanics and instrumentation unlike anything he had ever seen. Scattered chunks of a smooth substance that looked a little like plastic but wasn't, not quite. A weird stench, too, as of many things rotting and decayed.

He stared at it for a long time. He walked around the edge of it. The smell was from charred puddles of something rotting—so torn up now that it was hard to imagine what it had been when alive. Maybe the plane, if it was a plane, had crashed into a herd of deer and wiped them out. There were gouges in the ground and burn marks on the plasticine. From the bits and pieces it seemed like it was a plane of sorts, but no kind of plane he had ever seen. Probably some sort of spy plane or something. Probably the kind of thing a newspaper would pay good money to learn about.

It creeped him out to be standing there, not knowing exactly what he was seeing. He needed to get a little distance and think it through, see if he could determine what it was exactly, what it meant.

He found a rock and sat down. Taking out his bottle, he took another drink. Then another. That was helping, even if there wasn't much left. He screwed the cap back on and then accidentally fumbled the bottle, dropping it onto the ground. It hit with a splat. Not broken, then.

Bending forward he felt around for the bottle. But when he found it he also found something gelatinous and rubbery, which turned out to be Crak.

**006. CRAK AWOKE. ITS GAMBLE HAD PAID OFF. A POTENTIAL HOST HAD ARRIVED.**

Unlike Ch'rgak, Crak had no lexicon. It could not engage in the niceties of informing the potential host of the honor that was about to be bestowed upon it by becoming a host. All Crak could do was rapidly ooze up and over the appendage that had touched him and then quickly search and feel about looking for a way into the body. As Crak did this, Nichols was making loud sounds, and seemed to be trying to shake Crak off his appendage. Crak rapidly flowed upward and through the yellow-white filamental growth surrounding the head orifice and into the orifice itself.

A strong stench of chemicals and fermentation proceeded from said orifice. For a moment Crak hesitated, worried it was encountering an individual already serving as a host. Perhaps if Crak flowed in it would find Ch'rgak and Ch'ifi already there.

But what if Crak did? Crak had little choice: it needed a host. It would have to take the risk.

It slid down the chute within the mouth orifice and into Nichols' body. It plugged itself into the spinal column and began to delicately bore holes that would eventually allow its tentacles and feelers to protrude. It spread the chest bones wider and began to feed off what it judged by palpation to be the less necessary organs.

In the process, it absorbed all of contents of Nichols' stomach, which consisted of slightly north of half a bottle of whiskey.

Immediately, Crak began to feel nauseous. It turned itself inside out, but being within Nichols' body cavity meant that there was nowhere for the liquor to go, and with his innards exposed Crak absorbed it all the faster. The Nichols body stood and stumbled, as Crak sent Nichols lurching in the first direction he saw.

Suddenly Crak felt great numbness, and with this came a great warmth toward the being known as Nichols. As Crak propelled the Nichols body forward and back, test driving it, occasionally picking it up off the ground and starting it moving again, Crak began to have visions of itself not as it was now but as it would be once its status had been achieved through the conquering of this world. *Ch'rak,* the others of its kind would shout, *the great Ch'rak!* They would hold out their limb and sticky tentacles in obeisance and welcome. Or no, Crak thought, the name Ch'rak was not sufficient for its greatness. Crak would be great, one of the truly great, one of the chosen few. Crak would be not Ch'rak, but Ch'Ch'rak!

And then Crak froze. It was still awake, but it could no longer send commands to Nichols' spinal column. The body continued walking without him. Had Nichols regained control? No, not exactly: the consciousness of the host was still subdued. But the autonomic systems of the body seemed to have taken over. These were walking the Nichols/Crak creature somewhere. *Where?* wondered Crak. But before Crak could wonder further, it blacked out.

**007. WHEN CRAK AWOKE, IT WAS IN WHAT IT LEARNED FROM THE NICHOLS MEMORY SYSTEM WAS CALLED A BUSH.** The Nichols body was sleeping there. Was it usual for the Nichols body to sleep in a bush? It seemed so. Or at least not completely unusual.

Crak felt a pain in the Nichols leg. Something was prodding the body there. The Nichols eyes opened and through the green goggles covering them Crak saw a creature not dissimilar to Nichols, though without the white filamental growth around the head orifice.

Crak still had little control of the Nichols body, was still at least partly, though pleasantly, paralyzed. The Nichols consciousness still seemed largely subdued. But the Nichols body seemed able to function despite that. The Nichols body groaned and sat up.

"You slept here again?" said the voice of the man who had kicked Nichols. *McAlester*, the Nichols memory system drowsily informed him it was.

The Nichols head orifice did not vocalize, and yet this McAlester seemed to expect a response. Now that the body was activated, Crak, making a vast effort, managed to transmit a message to the brain, with the command to translate it into Nichols' language and extrude it through the head orifice.

"I did indeed partake of rest within the comfort known as a bush."

The expression on McAlester's face darkened. Consulting the Nichols brain, Crak realized this was not a positive omen.

"Quit screwing around. Get up, Nichols, get to the mine."

Again, Crak had little control as the body stood and began to drag its way forward.

Probably the substance that Nichols had drunk was incapacitating Crak. Probably Nichols had drunk it in error. Once the substance had completely evacuated his system, the body would be fine. Then Crak too would be fine, Crak would take charge, and would set about taking over this world. It was only a matter of time.

Crak flexed its neural net, readying it, waiting for the moment when it could again take control of the body.

**ON THE WAY TO THE MINE, NICHOLS'S HANDS BECAME AWARE OF THE BOTTLE IT HAD BEEN TIGHTLY GRASPING SINCE THE NIGHT BEFORE.** Unscrewing the cap, almost by reflex, he raised the bottle to his lips and took a big glug.

Inside, Crak felt its determination begin to waver. It became dizzy.

*All right*, Crak thought. *Not today. But soon. He can't drink forever. Soon he will have to stop. When he does I will take charge.*

But Nichols could, as it turned out, drink forever. Or at least for as long of forever as it took to pickle Crak and stop the last invader before conquest had really begun.

WHERE THE DEAD PEOPLE LIVE
BY CHRISTOPHER FARNSWORTH

Mr. Green returns home from his trip late. His wife is already asleep. A glass of wine and an Ambien and she is out cold by eleven. He knows her habits so well, but he still checks the bedroom for her gentle snores. He's not ready for bed yet, still wired from the coffee he drank and the hours on the road driving at high speed. He's up. So he figures, what the hell. He picks up the remote and fires up the TV.

He turns on the Serial Killer Channel.

The channel hides in the digital signals of most major cable systems, even though it only survives as a concession to the dinosaurs like himself. The younger guys prefer the dedicated web sites on the Dark Net or the Underweb or whatever. (Mr. Green has a Facebook account he never uses and answers emails grudgingly, and that is the extent of his technological savvy.) For the channel, he only has to press the number six three times on his remote. The TV providers are still superstitious about that. You're never going to have one of the ESPNs on a channel with the Mark of the Beast.

It's been a while since he's watched even though he's been a subscriber since it began. It hasn't changed much. There's a community-access feel to the logo that appears at the breaks, the video has a grainy quality, and the ads are written out, like classifieds, in a digital font that hasn't been used anywhere else for decades.

There are notices for freelance body disposal services, sales of high-quality blades and high-powered rifles, zip ties in bulk, and gently used white vans.

And there are the personals, like the ones that were once placed by people looking for love. Descriptions and ages and cities hanging on the screen long enough that anyone interested can get the relevant details and decide if he's willing to make the next move.

But these ads are not placed by the subjects. They're written by the hunters too old or infirm or respectable to do the work themselves now. They keep an eye out. You never lose the instincts. You can still smell weakness. Mr. Green can tell you that. (The profilers love to say that serial killers age out of the urge, that they go "quiescent" and give up the hunt after a number of years. It's a handy excuse for all the ones that get away, for the bodies found in landfills, the families that never get an answer to their grief. Boy, do they laugh at this at the annual Network conventions. Nobody gives it up willingly.)

One ad, in block digital text, reads:

*SWF, 30ish, div. w/no kids. Looking for love in all the wrong places. Multiple men, never stay for long. Careless w/keys and back patio door. No dog, no alarm. Fine set of Henckels knives on kitchen counter. Minneapolis. Msg. 612-XXX-XXX for address.*

Mr. Green yawns. Boring. Even if he was not fresh from a trip, this is not tempting enough to lure him out again.

The channel started back in the 80s, as one young hunter, a tech at a regional cable company, convinced a majority of the members that the Network magazine was becoming too great a risk. It depended on the mail, and no matter how many fake names or P.O. Boxes you used, there was always the chance those pages would be opened to the wrong eyes, like a nosy neighbor, or a prying letter carrier, or a child digging through Dad's nightstand, looking for a copy of *Playboy*.

So the tech created a channel that could only be accessed by those who knew where to look. In the first days, Mr. Green remembers having to press down two buttons at the same time on his old cable box, then dial the tuner carefully until the picture came in clear.

(The profilers cannot believe that this level of organization exists among them, or even that Mr. Green and his kind can maintain families. The profilers prefer to think they cannot form lasting attachments, that they lack the internal resources to hold a steady job, to marry and have children, to gain status and position in any kind of normal community. They point to bedwetters and whiners like Bundy and Berkowitz to prove it. When someone like poor old Dennis Rader comes along and blows that theory out of the water, they say he's the exception that proves the rule. Mr. Green finds it sad, really. All those hardworking FBI men have no idea how many of them hold it together perfectly well all their living days, only adding to the numbers of the dead when there is no chance of getting caught. They live comfortably in the authorities' blind spots, invisible because no one believes they exist. He has met CEOs, priests, softball coaches, surgeons, high school principals, hedge fund managers, and HVAC repairmen who share his hobby. They've compared pictures and trophies and stories over drinks. Altogether, he finds them no less well-adjusted than the men who march into the woods with high-powered rifles to kill Bambi every fall.)

Once the ads are done, the videos resume. It looks like Mr. Green caught a good night. There are no hosts, no commentary, no frills. Just raw images taken by the men—and yes, it's almost always men—who do the work. They used to mail in tapes, and now they send clips from the cameras on burner phones. Here is a video from a newcomer who recorded the last 14 minutes in the life of a young woman tied to a chair in his garage. She begs and pleads as her killer uses a knife to slice away her clothing—not really Mr. Green's preference, to be honest—but soon devolves into a shrieking animal, the tears and blood and sweat all running down her face. Her mouth distends while her cries merge into a single howl of pain. He turns down the volume, even though it would take a truck crashing into the house to wake his wife. He is careful. It's how he's lasted so long.

(Mr. Green has been married to the same woman for almost forty years. He built a successful contracting business and then shifted into development. Now he's semi-retired, lives in a nice little three-bedroom by a golf course. He raised three sons who went on to full, prosperous lives. [Well, except for Robert, but that's hardly Mr. Green's fault.] He rarely drinks or raises his voice in anger. He has a gold card and donates to charity and tips exactly 17 percent.)

The cheap phone's camera zooms in, blurring the picture for moment, and Mr. Green frowns, but then the video snaps back into focus, and the woman's face fills the screen. She's not pretty at this point. Perhaps she never was. But the young killer has talent, because he catches the most important seconds of her life. Mr. Green can see the light go out in her eyes as she loses all hope, when she knows that she is going to die, and there is only pain for however long she has left. That's the moment he loves, the stripping away of all the pretense, the collapse of the façade. That's where all the notions about soul and spirit and love and dignity fall apart, and all that is left is the brutal truth of nerves singing their response to external stimuli. This is where the meat is revealed.

(It's a balancing act. That's all. Like everything else in this life, you pick and choose. You don't say you're a Clippers fan to the guy wearing a Lakers shirt. You don't talk about politics with your Republican boss if you're a Democrat. You don't discuss religion with your neighbor who goes to that church that might as well be a cult. You only reveal your true self to the right people at the right time. The rest of your life is playacting, but it's not hard. Everyone does it.)

The next clip is disappointing by comparison. There is a lot of unnecessary knife work, too many lingering shots of the naked body of the victim. (Again, that has never been Mr. Green's thing, the sex part that seems to motivate so many of his kind. He has no problem with normal relations. He doesn't even need Cialis.) There is all kinds of heavy breathing and background chatter. Ridiculous. This guy is amateurish and stupid. If he lasts more than three or four kills, Mr. Green will be shocked. He's leaving his signature all over, practically spray-painting clues on the wall for some half-bright detective to find.

It leaves a bad taste in Mr. Green's mouth. He suspects whoever does the programming for the channel runs these kinds of clips the same way other TV stations run old sitcoms with their predictable setups and canned laugh tracks. But he doesn't like them. They remind him of the stereotypes about his kind. It's almost as insulting as the network dramas about bad guys brought to justice every week by heroic cops.

He's not dumb enough to want credit—that's one hair away from being one of those guys who *wants* to get caught—but Jesus, the sheer idiocy of it all. Is there no one capable of doing the basic math? Roughly 600,000 people go missing every year in the United States. And—because

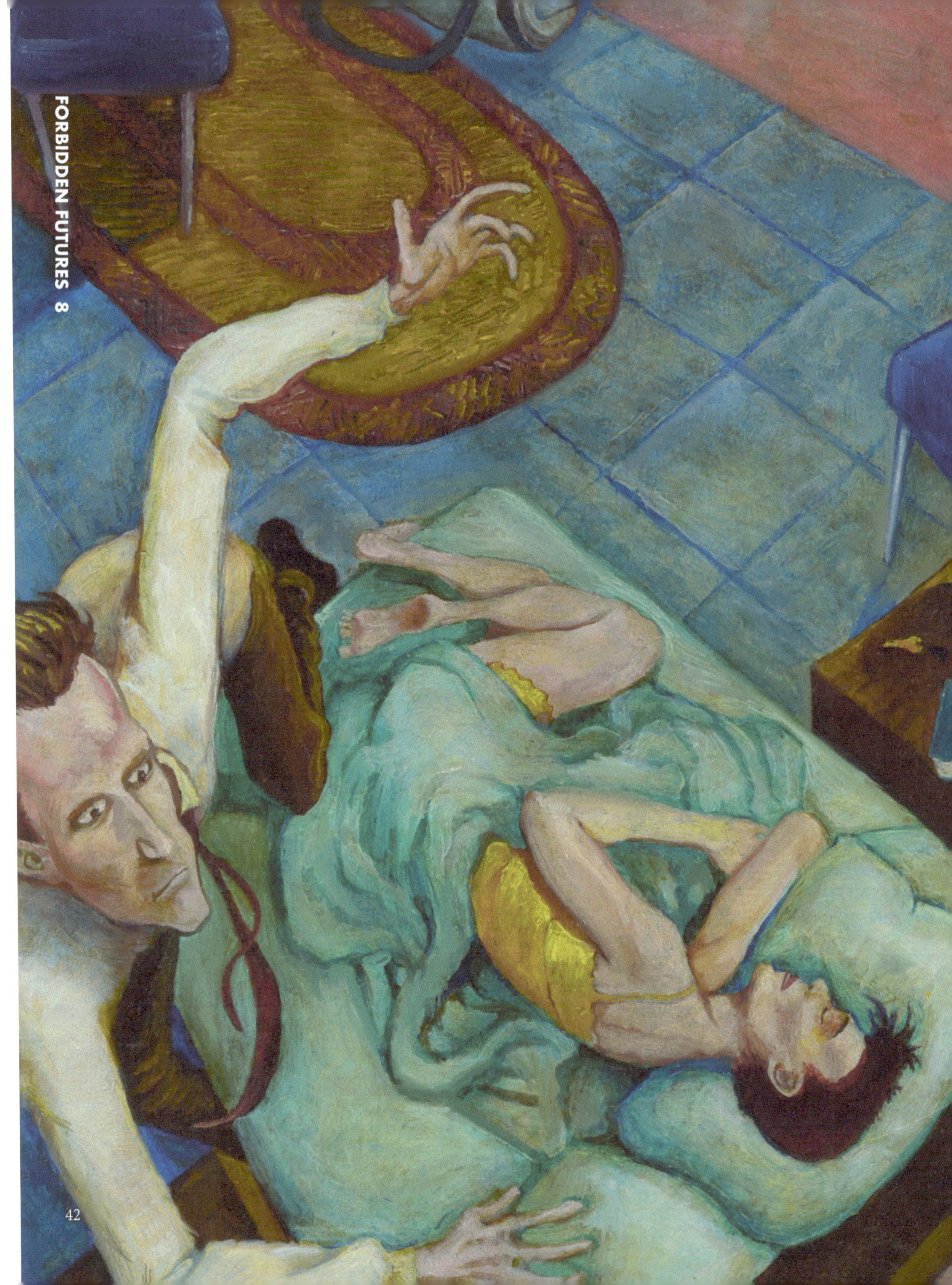

most police departments are unequipped to handle any murder that doesn't involve the killer standing over the victim with a bloody knife in his hand— about a third of all murders in America now go unsolved. (Homicides used to have a clearance rate of 90 percent. Mr. Green keeps up with the statistics.)

Even when you account for all the people who come wandering home after a couple weeks in Vegas, there are a lot of dead people out there. Mr. Green used to wonder, doesn't the imbalance in the ledger ever occur to anyone else? Doesn't anyone ever wonder, *Hey, what happens to all those thousands of people who vanish every year?*

No. Nobody cares. The cops are overworked and understaffed. They can barely find all the people who owe money for speeding tickets. Someone leaves town, it's one less problem for them.

And the families? Well, Mr. Green has never stuck around for the funerals—that's another rookie mistake—but he suspects they are relieved, deep down. It is easier to deal with a memory than the messy reality of an actual human being. If you remove Uncle Rudy from everyone's daily life, it's possible to forget he was actually sort of a pain in the ass who borrowed money and made the same bad jokes every Thanksgiving. One less name on the Christmas card list. One less birthday to remember.

That's the beauty of it. Nobody really wants to know what happened to all those dead people, piling up every year.

Nobody but Mr. Green and his kind. They have built a national apparatus, an infrastructure for disposing of the surplus of humanity. It is a public service, in some ways; a form of population control. They have their own organization, the Network, with meetings, customs, even their own forms of currency. Jesus Christ, they have *group discount cards*. There is no way to deal with the sheer number of the dead without all of this. They find and recruit their own kind, fill their ranks with more every year. They have built a machine that turns people into memories. And there is a place for them, because they are necessary.

They are the last ones who care. They are the only ones who want to know where the dead people go. They are the only ones who actually appreciate these men and women and boys and girls in the final seconds of their lives.

(This is the fact that the profilers will never understand. They love to make their models and write their books—he's read them all—as if murder can be diagrammed like an electrical circuit. He's sure some of them are smart, but they all engage in the same fallacy, and they don't even see it. They talk about *shallow affect* and *failure of empathy* and *adrenaline tolerance* and even *lack of conscience*, but those are all scientific dress-up for ideas laid down in the Old Testament. They think that people ought to be treated differently than every other animal on the planet. They persist in the illusion that there is a void inside people like him, a hollow place where whatever they now call the soul should live.)

Mr. Green knows economics. A thing is only worth what someone else is willing to pay for it. He and his kind are the only people in America who really value a human life.

(The truth is there's no intrinsic value to any person. There's no alarm that goes off when you kill another human being. He's never seen anything like the soul escape from a dying body, no matter how close he's been. And he's been very close.)

And that is why the channel exists, aside from the obvious reasons of entertainment and vanity and nostalgia and boredom. This is where the dead people live, one last time. This is where the actual point of their lives is revealed. There's something important about that, Mr. Green thinks. Something that should be preserved, even if most of the world will never see it.

Mr. Green experiences a small moment of déjà vu as the next video fills the screen. He knows this muddy riverbank, this bend in the current, this brown water. His pulse quickens, and fear squirts through him for an instant, as if there are the lights of a police car in his rear-view mirror.

But then he understands.

This is his video. The one he couldn't resist sending in, years ago.

It's the only time he felt he had to keep a record. There were many times he used the camera, which he kept in a black garbage bag in the trunk of his car, but he would always erase the tapes. Except for this one.

She was a runner, and strong, and she fought, which is perhaps why he wanted to remember her. She valued her own life.

But no, that's not it. They all did. Whether they begged or fought or went still with terror, they all wanted to live.

She nearly got away. That was all.

He'd set up the camera, believing her to be incapacitated from the first stab wound, the one he was always careful to place in the lung, under the rib, so they couldn't breathe properly or shout. Then, when he came close again, she sprang to life, and kicked. She got him hard in the crotch and stars danced in his eyes. She leaped up and began stumbling away from him, clutching her side.

For a moment, he saw it all come undone, his careful life, his unbroken string of triumphs. He saw her in an emergency room, surrounded by doctors and nurses, giving the police a detailed description of the man who did this.

In desperation, he flung himself forward, reaching as far as he could, and his fingers came into contact with her ankle.

He grabbed, and even though he lost his grip, it was enough to trip her up. She slipped down the grassy bank, and fell under him.

He came down with the knife, and it was over quickly, although he didn't stop stabbing her for some time.

The camera caught it all, and he decided it was an object lesson for others. He wanted them to see it. To let them know, you could do it all right, plan it all perfectly, and still have to depend on a lucky moment to save you.

(There is no punishment, no divine retribution, no karma, no justice. You might as well wait for Superman to show up and save the day at the last minute. Or aliens. The truth is, there is us, and there is them. There is the butcher and there is the meat. And we can do whatever we want to them as long as we get away with it. There is no one to stop us. Mr. Green knows.)

His face is not really visible in the video. He always wore a hood and a baseball cap and a bandanna around his face. He doesn't even look much like that anymore. But he's still a little proud of that younger man, that stronger man, the one who never needed a gun, who could lift a body into the trunk of a car without grunting or straining—

"Grandpa?"

He clicks the TV off instantly.

He turns and sees his grandson, Matty. Mr. Green should have checked the guest bedroom.

"Grandpa, what were you watching?"

The kid looks scared. Of course he does. He's scared of everything. He stays with them at least once a week while his mother goes out looking for a man to replace Mr. Green's son Robert.

Robert was worthless. This is not Mr. Green's fault. He raised his son right. His other boys are both fine men. But not Robert. Robert was always "sensitive," which was his wife's word for weak. He ended his own life in a drunken car crash not long after Matty was born.

People wondered what made Robert such a mess. Mr. Green had no answers for them.

(He does not like to think about the times he saw Robert looking at him, even as a child, with a kind of terrible understanding on his face. There was no way Robert knew. But he looked as if he did. It troubled Mr. Green. It troubled him even more as Robert tried harder to hide it, the older he got.)

Now Matty looks at him.

"How much did you see?" he says, and he knows it comes out all wrong, too sharp and too insistent.

Matty flinches. He doesn't answer.

"It's okay," he says, putting his best smile on his face. "Come here."

He holds his arms out for a hug, but Matty doesn't move from his spot on the carpet. The little bastard usually clings like a goddamn monkey, and now he won't come near him.

"What were you watching?" Matty asks again, his voice higher and tighter now. Mr. Green takes a deep breath.

"I'm sorry," he says, keeping his voice warm and even. "I was watching a horror movie on TV. Grown-up stuff. Too scary for you. I hope you didn't see too much. It will give you nightmares."

Matty doesn't say anything. He takes a step back.

Mr. Green tries to remember how old he is now. Six? You can tell a three, or a four-year-old, or even a kid who's five, that they didn't see something, and they'll believe you. They won't even remember what they saw, half the time. He knows this from experience.

"For a second, I thought—" Matty says. He hesitates. He doesn't want to say it.

"You thought you saw something pretty bad, didn't you?" Mr. Green says.

Matty nods, tears in his eyes. He's terrified. For a second, Mr. Green sees it all fall apart again. He sees Matty pressing buttons on the remote until he finds the hidden channel. He sees the child telling his mother. He sees questions, accumulated like fine dust over the years, suddenly shaking loose all at once.

"It was me," Mr. Green says.

Matty's eyes go wide.

"It wasn't you," Mr. Green says quickly. "It wasn't your fault. It was me. I shouldn't have been watching a scary movie like that, and I'm sorry it woke you up. You didn't do anything wrong. You're not in trouble, Matty. It was me. It was all my fault."

Mr. Green opens his arms again.

"You're okay," he says. "You're safe."

Matty stands there for a moment, on the edge. He wants to believe. Mr. Green can see it. He wants to believe in the man who gives him presents and takes him out for donuts and lets him drive the golf cart sometimes. He doesn't want to believe his own eyes. He wants to trust. He wants his grandpa.

Matty smiles, and the tears roll down his face, and he rushes into his grandfather's arms.

Mr. Green hugs him close, and strokes his back, and says, over and over, "It's all right. You're safe."

Matty chokes back his tears. Mr. Green can feel him pull it together. The kid really is trying. He has to give him credit for that.

He looks up at Mr. Green, and the tension is gone. He curls into Mr. Green's chest happily.

"Feel better?" Mr. Green asks.

He nods.

"We should get you to bed," Mr. Green says. "Your mom will be really mad at me if she knows I let you stay up late watching horror movies."

Matty laughs. It's a joke now. It's getting farther away from real every second.

And it's a secret. Between the two of them.

"Okay," Matty says.

He's seven. Mr. Green remembers. The candle on the cake was shaped like a seven last year.

Too old.

"Hey," he says, as if the thought has just occurred to him. "Why don't you and I head down to the river tomorrow? Take a walk. Just you and me."

Matty nods, yawns, almost asleep in his lap now. "Sure," he says. "That sounds great."

"Good."

Mr. Green can feel the boy's pulse in his neck under his fingers.

"I love you, Grandpa," he says.

"I love you, too, Matty."

(It's a balancing act. Like everything else in this life. That's all.)

**RUDY RUCKER** is a mathematician, a computer scientist, an artist, and the author of more than forty books.  He worked for twenty years as a professor of computer science in Silicon Valley.  He received Philip K. Dick awards for his cyberpunk Software and Wetware. His most recent novel is Million Mile Road Trip.  See also his Complete Stories. Nine of his novels were reissued by Night Shade in 2019. Rudy blogs at www.rudyrucker.com/blog

**MIKE DUBISCH** began his lifetime career in illustration and comics while still in high school, coloring comics for every major studio while writing and publishing his own short graphic works for publication. The artist never stopped exploring the subjects he enjoyed in these young years- Fantastic worlds and bizarre creatures, dynamic warriors and exotic females- and has since contributed to the worlds of Star Wars, Dungeons and Dragons, and Aliens VS Predator. Working with author Tom Simmons, Mike is in the final stages of adapting a long out of print Edgar Rice Burroughs novel in web comic form. His work in films and book illustration is well known by fans of the Cthulhu Mythos of H.P. Lovecraft. Lately Mike has concentrated on exploring his personal obsessions and traveling the world on location sketching in Morocco, Mexico, Latin America and the UK, while teaching on-line at the Academy Of University in San Francisco. See more at MikeDubisch.com

**EVAN J. PETERSON** created Drag Star!, the world's first drag performer RPG. His writing appears in Weird Tales, Queers Destroy Horror, Nightmare Magazine, & Best Gay Stories 2015. A Clarion West alum, he founded the SHRIEK: Women of Horror Film series in 2015. Forthcoming works include the serial novel Better Living Through Alchemy and a superhero RPG.

**BRIAN EVENSON** was praised by Peter Straub for going "furthest out on the sheerest, least sheltered narrative precipice," Brian Evenson is the recipient of three O. Henry Prizes and has been a finalist for the Edgar Award, the Shirley Jackson Award, and the World Fantasy Award. He is also the winner of the International Horror Guild Award and the American Library Association's award for Best Horror Novel, and his work has been named in Time Out New York's top books.

**PHILIP FRACASSI** is an award-winning author and screenwriter. His debut collection of stories, BEHOLD THE VOID, is available in ebook, paperback, audiobook and hardcover, and was named "Story Collection of the Year (2017)" by THIS IS HORROR. His stories have appeared in multiple magazines and anthologies, including BEST HORROR OF THE YEAR VOLUME TEN and NIGHTMARE MAGAZINE. His work has been reviewed by The New York Times, Rue Morgue Magazine, LOCUS Magazine and others. His screenplay credits include "Girl Missing," distributed by Lifetime Television and "Santa Paws 2: The Santa Pups," distributed by Disney Entertainment. Philip lives with his family in Los Angeles, California.

**CODY GOODFELLOW** has written eight novels. His latest are GRIDLOCKED (King Shot Press) and SCUM OF THE EARTH (Eraserhead Press). His books, SILENT WEAPONS FOR QUIET WARS and ALL-MONSTER ACTION, and UNAMERICA received the Wonderland Book Award. As an actor, he has appeared in numerous short films, TV shows, music videos and commercials. He "lives" in Portland, OR.

**S.G. MURPHY** is a nonbinary trans woman from the eastern continental US. She is the author of the 2019 story collection "The Worst That Could Happen" and enjoys cooking, working on cars, and the sound of distant gunfire."

**JONATHAN RAAB** is the author of Flight of the Blue Falcon, The Hillbilly Moonshine Massacre, The Lesser Swamp Gods of Little Dixie, and Camp Ghoul Mountain Part VI: The Official Novelization. His short fiction has appeared in the Lovecraft eZine, The Book of Blasphemous Words, Letters of Decline, A Breath From the Sky, and Turn to Ash Volume 2: Open Lines. His nonfiction has appeared in the New York Times At War blog, CNN.com, Stars and Stripes, and others. He lives in Colorado with his wife, son, and their dog Egon.

**ELIZABETH RAYNE** is a she-writer owned by a parrot. When not writing, she can most likely be found cosplaying as a character nobody ever heard of.

**CAROLYN WATSON DUBISCH** is an artist, illustrator, sculptor and author. In her years as a professional artist she's created giant vegetables for a Washington DC Museum, helped create two dozen tiny hot air balloons for a Vegas show and designed alien bird-men for Star Wars games.

**CHRISTOPHER FARNSWORTH** is a novelist, screenwriter, and journalist. He is the author of FLASHMOB, KILLFILE, THE ETERNAL WORLD, and the President's Vampire series, as well as the comic book 24: LEGACY -- RULES OF ENGAGEMENT. His books have been translated into nine languages, published in more than a dozen countries, and optioned for film and television. His writing has also been published by the Los Angeles Times, the New York Post, The Awl, and The New Republic. He lives in Los Angeles with his wife and daughters. You can find out more at www.christopherfarnsworth.com.